BIG JOHN AND THE ISLAND OF BONES

DUKE TATE

CONTENTS

1

RUM AND HABANOS

Thursday, October 22nd

Big John arrived at the Cuban Coffee Queen's eatery stand, a thatched grey wooden shack with a black menu over to the right, and ordered two shots of *bucci* (or espresso) with sugar – the classic Cuban coffee. The woman, as Cuban as the coffee, with smooth olive skin and a low-cut shirt, served him the buccis in two small plastic sauce containers – one for each shot. He took the shots back slowly and went to sit on the old weathered wooden bench nearby to smoke a Cohiba Habano he had tucked into the pocket of his midnight-blue linen shirt pocket. A dark red chicken walked by, pecking at the ground. The October sun was a steaming 81 degrees – fall in the Keys. His friend, Eduardo, scored him the Habanos by the box once a month from Cuba and although John had mainly received donations for his healing work over the last four years, his extensive list of patients had left him with quite a pile of cash, so he could afford the luxury.

Key West, Cayo Hueso or Bone Key or even better, the Island of Bones, as it was also known to the locals, was called the Cigar Capital of the World in the 19th and early 20th century. One hundred million cigars were hand-rolled there in one year. A place of the senses where rum flowed like water and everything was always in bloom, the 103-mile proximity to Cuba made the small island a popular spot for rum running in the Prohibition years, and the Conchs (a name given to the natives) had gotten a taste for the sweet liquor that never left their palate.

Since moving from Big Sur to Key West three months ago, Big John had taken pride in his share of the stimulants. He was taking three or four coffees a day, a cigar or two in the middle and Ron Zacapa dark Guatemalan rum in the evenings, poured over a single fat square of ice.

His lovely wife, Angela, whose smooth Thai skin now glowed with a sweet richness from the hot Key West sun, took a little rum and a bucci or two a day, but nothing like John. She preferred the island's coconut water served in the nut with a straw and Key Lime Pie – the luscious concoction of sugar, eggs and condensed milk sent her to the moon. Always paranoid about his weight, John rarely touched the pie, but did take his share of the coconut juice. Besides, Angela loved running her fingers over his rock-solid abs these days and he wouldn't change that for all the pie in America.

After smoking the Cuban slow and hard, and finishing the coffee, John walked over to the docks where he found Dan, his saltwater flats fly-fishing guide. A chubby guy sitting on his fishing-boat chair, Dan was a brown-bearded man with mocha skin, Costa del Mar sunglasses with blue reflective lenses, and a trucker hat with a baby blue tarpon on it. He had migrated south to the Keys six years ago from Ocean Springs, Mississippi, in search of warmer weather, driven by the lure of his own salty piece of land.

John shook Dan's hand and Dan welcomed him aboard. They set off into the blazing sun and in under an hour reached the mangrove bushes. John started sightfishing on the fly for small tarpon and bonefish using a double haul cast, where the left hand pulls the slack out of the line before the right hand raises the rod up, and then the left pulls back up and down on the line again when the cast is in the air.

Through the crystal-clear water, John could see down to the rocky bottom. Enormous brown stingrays floated mysteriously underneath the rippling water, appearing like undulating rocks as they moved. Being bold and hungry for the sun, John removed his Grateful Dead khaki-colored hat with the blue dancing bear stitched on the front. He was wearing midnight-blue swim trunks patterned with lime-green palm trees. Stubborn as a mule, John hated sunscreen and only used coconut oil on his skin. Within four hours, his face always turned a smooth red hue, which he loved.

Dan and he spotted many bonefish, barracuda, sting rays, permit and even a hogfish – a local delicacy – but got skunked on the take. A cold front had moved in three days before and the temperature had dropped to a cool 68 degrees in the daytime, and although the weather was warm again, the fish hadn't moved back in. Back at the docks, John paid Dan, slipping him a roll of hundreds for his troubles and thanking him for the outing.

A FIERY AFFAIR

After John left the marina, Dan wandered over to Alonzo's Oyster House at the Key West Marina with a face full of sun from fishing, ordered a dirty gin martini and a large tower of oysters and started drinking. He lit a Lucky Brand unfiltered cigarette – he only smoked Lucky's because he was obsessed with the movie *Key Largo*, in which Edward G. Robinson's character was loosely based on gangsters Lucky Luciano and Al Capone – and smoked it slowly while flirting with Donna, the waitress with no last name who he was hoping to take home with him that night. But she wouldn't budge. He kept drinking, hoping to get her number. By 6:30 pm he was drunk and loading his boat into his trailer.

Thirty minutes later he was driving down the highway without Donna, listening to "Bad, Bad Leroy Brown" by Jim Croce while smoking a cigarette. When he finished the butt, he flipped it out the window. The wind caught the butt and it landed in the back of the boat, near the engine.

Some fuel had leaked out right next to the cigarette and when the butt rolled a little with the movement of the truck, the fuel ignited, catching the boat on fire. Dan was so drunk, it took a moment for him to notice it, and by that time the whole thing was ablaze.

Officer Hank Judge saw the flame sear past him in a flash as the truck was going 50 mph at the time. He flipped his siren on and roared after Dan, who was already making his way to the side of the road up ahead.

Officer Judge waited behind the parked truck and called for backup and a fire squad. Meanwhile, Dan hopped out of the truck stomping his feet on the ground, paranoid he might be on fire also.

A moment later, two fire trucks arrived and extinguished the fire on the boat. Dan sat there shaking his head, wondering how in the hell his boat could have caught fire from a cigarette butt. Lucky no more, he thought, staring at the stupid empty pack of cigarettes.

By Hank's squad car, Dan was interviewed at length before failing a field sobriety test. He was booked for drunk driving and hauled in: his fourth Driving Under the Influence offense (DUI).

Back in his car, Hank Judge smiled at the sheer hilarity of the whole event. Before pulling out, he received an emoji from Maggie with a wink and a tongue sticking out. He smiled in disbelief. Maggie of all people – his high school crush.

"Hey Hank, so what you doing?"

"Nut and honey," he typed, referencing the commercial for 1980s cereal brand, Nut & Honey.

"Hahaha," she texted.

"Just down here in Key West, enforcing the law. What about you? Still a model in L.A.?"

"No, I quit it all a few years back. I'm in Vermont now. Listen, funny you should say that, I'm on my way to the Keys in a few days for a break. Want to hang out?"

"Sure babe! Why don't you stay with me while you're at it?"

"Really? Could I?"

"Yeah, of course!"

3

THROAT PROBLEMS

On the way home from the marina, the rain moved in as John snaked his jet-black 1995 Land Rover Defender through the streets of downtown Key West. Halloween was in full flush and houses were decorated with the typical pumpkins for the carving and with skeletons, one wearing old sailor fatigue along with a captain's hat.

When he pulled into Angela and his white clapboard rental cottage at 121 Caroline Street, he unloaded the two warty pumpkins he had just bought on the side of the road onto the front porch. Their Northern Inuit puppy, Howlin' Wolf – named after the legendary Mississippi blues musician – greeted him. He looked vaguely like John's white wolf who used to be his spirit guide back in Big Sur. John pet Howlin' Wolf, calling him "big man", and then strutted into the kitchen.

John received a text from Angela, claiming she had taken the Jeep into town for groceries. "Ah," John thought. "Delicious Thai food tonight, wonder what it will be... yummy."

He turned on the coffee maker and loaded it with Jamaican Blue Mountain for a change. He drank half a cup and sat down in front of his iMac by the window in his home office overlooking Caroline Street, and began typing faster than he had ever typed in his life.

After ten minutes, he paused to sip the black coffee out of his favorite white mug lettered with black bold script, "Coffee or Bust", while the Key West rain nailed the tin roof of the cottage.

For the last couple of months since moving to Florida, Big John had been writing a "How To" book on how others could channel energy through their palms to help individuals with their health, just like he did. His ability to cure people from all manner of illnesses with his palms, even from a distance via Skype, had made him an anomaly for the last four years for clients all over the world.

Angela and he had been living at an off-grid address in Big Sur, California, that few people – even their closest friends – knew about, so they could protect John's gift in privacy. In many ways, he had become a hermit over the years, a recluse due to his notoriety, and many people had even forgotten what he looked like.

Three months ago, his spirit guide, the white wolf that Angela and he had come across that day on Nepenthe beach many years ago, darted off into the Redwood forest, never to return again. Heavyhearted, he decided to take a sabbatical from working on patients, buy a Northern Inuit puppy, and rent a little cottage in Key West – an enclave for artists and writers alike – to work on a book to help others find their own gift.

He thought that perhaps just by walking the very streets where fellow writers had lived, he might catch the writing bug. And it worked – the words flowed out of him in such a staggering ensemble that he estimated the book would end up being the size of a colossal bookend.

Since starting the book, black coffee had become John's best friend. Lately, he even dreamed about it in the evenings. Coffee had become an obsession; his favorite hobby had become creeping down the aisle at Sandra's Organic Market up the street to whiff all the various beans from different countries. He knew them all by smell, each one uniquely different: Jamaican, Italian, French, African, Brazilian, Peruvian. Then there were the different notes of chicory, such as dark roast and espresso. He liked strong, bold aromas. It was why he loved his wife Angela's Thai food – because of the robust flavors.

Starbucks' nitro cold brew was his newest kick when Angela and he were crawling Duval Street (known as the longest street in America because it stretches 1.2 miles from the Gulf of Mexico to the Atlantic), especially after a drink or two, because the nitrogen caused the caffeine to process more slowly in his body. And of course, he loved his Cuban buccis on their front porch in his white rocking chair with a real Cuban cigar. In a pinch, such as on a long road trip to Saint Augustine near the Georgia state line, he happily slurped down a Folgers or watered-down gas-station coffee, but he was now a coffee snob at heart, leaning more toward the puritanical side of addicts: never a Frappuccino guy – those were for teenage girls and lightweights, John believed a real man took his coffee like he took his whiskey – dark and strong.

Perhaps at some level he had slowly swapped addictions without really knowing it – his former bad food addiction for coffee and cigars. He didn't like soda either: too much sugar, and the buzz just wasn't there. Tea was good in a crunch, he could get a half buzz going on a 16-ounce green tea, but it couldn't really put him in the zone. For that, he needed old faithful: the go-to choice for cowboys on the range and police officers alike.

Coffee opened the world to him. Right after that first blazing hot sip in his white rocker on the porch, overlooking Caroline every morning at the butt crack of dawn, he wanted to study for hours. He wanted to learn, he wanted to know about history, civilizations and the world. It amplified his spotlight thinking (analytical thought).

My goodness, where was this miracle juice when he was studying in high school? Adults guarded their coffee secret like some mystical scroll with the meaning of life scribbled on it. They didn't want kids to know about the magic beans that allowed you to climb to the clouds. Hell, after a cup, Big John might even enjoy looking at some statistics for hours.

But there was a downside. He felt too nervous, his heart beat irregularly, he was too hot, his neck was sore and tight after just one cup and he was often scatterbrained. Sipping again from his mug, he typed for another thirty minutes, but something unfamiliar happened when he reached the 100th page. He stopped being able to write. It didn't matter what John did, he simply couldn't proceed. His mind was blank.

Antsy, he opened his Rosewood cigar humidor, gently picked up a Cuban cigar off the Spanish cedar tray and walked out to the front porch where he blazed it. He sat there, contemplatively watching the rain fall. Like many weather systems in the Keys, in ten minutes the rain had moved on. While enjoying his buzz, he noticed that his throat was ever so slightly constricted. Strange, he thought, glancing at the cigar.

He didn't try to heal himself with his magic hands. He knew he couldn't – the one curse of his gift was his inability to cure himself from any illness with his special hands. Although he rarely got sick, at times like these when he had a problem, he never knew what to do. He needed to find another healer like him, but there weren't any, or at least he didn't know about any if they existed.

His book would change that, he hoped. He saw a world full of healers able to cure the worst maladies after it was released.

Shortly afterwards, Angela swung her white Jeep into the driveway and got out quickly in a steam of humidity. She looked stunning in her pink tank top with her long black hair pulled back into a ponytail and her cut jean shorts and black leather thongs. So natural and full of life.

"Hey babe," she said.

"Hey sexy!" He snuffed out his cigar. "Need a hand?"

"Sure, come help."

"Alright." He hopped up, forgetting about his throat for a moment, hustled down the porch steps and wrangled over to the Jeep backdoor with a smile.

"Here you go, soldier," she said, handing him two bags.

"Sure babe!" He took them and carried them inside. Angela followed and Howlin' Wolf greeted them at the door, enthusiastically wagging his tail. His wolf-like eyes were that of a sailor who longed for the shore: sad in a humorous way. Those eyes always made the two lovers smile. They set the bags down on the kitchen island in the middle of their lilac-colored kitchen with Howlin' Wolf following.

Digging through the bags, John spotted the galangal and lemongrass and asked, "Are we having my favorite Thai Panang tonight?"

"You got it!" Angela smiled and pinched his butt as she walked past him on her way to the sink with the pork roast, and he hit her butt playfully. "But you promise we can cook out tomorrow on the grill and make steaks?" she asked, her head turned to him in a loving way.

"Of course, of course! Anything for you."

"Thanks babe. How was fishing today?"

"Good, I mean we got skunked, but hey, it's fishing! I always have fun!"

"Attaboy!"

While Angela prepared the pork for the oven, John waltzed over to their little bamboo bar cart, took a glass, and dropped in a diesel square ice cube from the ice bucket. "Think we'll have rain tomorrow?" he asked.

"Maybe."

He screwed the top off the Zacapa rum and poured a fatty glass. Then, he turned on Ibrahim Ferrer's "Oye el Consejo" on their wireless beach stereo and started dancing over to his lady. After taking a few quick sips of the rum, he set the glass on the island and took Angela's hand, twirling her around in the kitchen a few times. She laughed and they both smiled widely. Howlin' Wolf barked.

"Oh jeez, you smell like a cigar factory babe, you have to go shower, right this minute!" she ordered, pushing his chest away.

"Aww baby, do I really?"

"Yes, it's too strong love. You know I don't like that smell!"

4

M.M

Monday, October 26th

M.M. applied her red *Make Me Blush*-shade lipstick to her lush lips while studying her appearance in her pocket mirror by the window of the plane. She then removed her blue mirrored Ray Ban Aviator sunglasses and quickly stuffed them into her navy Patagonia travel purse before taking another sip of her bottled water.

She kept flirting with the guy next to her, Tim. He had long, wavy brown hair parted over to one side and thin, clear spectacles. His blue gingham shirt was driving her mad. There was certainly no one as posh as him in Applebury, Vermont where she lived. He reminded her of the hunks she used to pose with back in her modeling days in L.A.

The pilot came on in a southern accent announcing, "Ladies and gentlemen, we are making our final approach into Key West from New York, La Guardia."

M.M. had been her modeling name in L.A., but her birthname was Maggie May. She changed her name after it had been too colonial for her agent, Max Sparks. Maggie and Big

John had flirted some and almost hooked up in high school. She was his crush and the sole reason he had wandered into Madame Bernadette's fortune-telling shop in Venice, California that fateful day.

After John cured the crippled black boy on the 3rd Street Promenade with his magical hands, everything had changed. He had lost interest in Maggie, and although she pursued him heavily for a while, eventually she started seeing a French runway model named Gusto. John started dating Angela, and the two lovers eventually moved to Big Sur on the Central Coast of California.

After working as a high-paid model for a few years, Maggie finally grew sick of the appearance culture in the industry. One day, she just snapped, quit Hollywood, packed her baby blue Bentley GTC convertible in a frenzy with all her things from her cute Santa Monica apartment, and drove across the country to Applebury, Vermont near Burlington, where she had always wanted to live. She'd had a wild obsession with the place ever since visiting there when she was a little girl.

The day she pulled into Applebury after driving over a timber-trussed covered red bridge on a New England country road draped in autumn leaves, she felt at home, and knew it, and she had been there ever since.

Over time though, the demons from her past crept up with her, and one chilly October day in Vermont, in a manic daze she tried to drown herself in Lake Champlain by tying some bricks around her waist. Fortunately, a young guy out fishing on the lake saw her and saved her life.

During her two-week stay at the local mental hospital, she realized that when she was younger, a fellow classmate called Nicki Singer had tried to drown her in the neighborhood pool. Nicki held her blonde hair under so long, Maggie thought she would never let her up. When she finally did, Maggie was gasping for air. After that day, she became obsessed with water.

She drank more than most kids and lived to swim and be near the ocean. Gradually over time, she had forgotten about the incident. But in the dark recesses of her soul, it hadn't forgotten her, and was the very reason she tried to drown herself.

That day her life changed for the better.

Henceforth, she had decided to become a seer, and after her stay at the hospital, she began working at the Applebury Psychic Shop. It sold incense, tarot cards, Ouija boards, dowsing rods and other odd things of an esoteric nature. Maggie loved all of it. She spent her spare time communicating with spirits and sipping English tea in a nook by the window of Beans & Books with an out-of-print hardcover on magic spells or astrological signs.

When men walked in and saw the former drop-dead gorgeous blonde model working at the shop, they became believers in the supernatural as well.

Lately, the overcast Burlington weather had taken its toll on Maggie's mental health and she needed a break. She needed the sun. Starving for vitamin D, she decided to take a vacation to Key West down in Florida where an old high school buddy, Hank Judge, lived.

5

MR. DELGADO

October 31st, 1872

At 709 Truman Avenue, at the Queen Anne-style mansion built in 1870, Mr. Delgado slowly puffed his cigar, the sweet smell filling the room off the pool, while he sat with his legs crossed in a bamboo chair. An unusual chilly evening for Key West, a cool breeze wafted in through the opened window. A cigar baron, Mr. Delgado loved the taste of his own cigars, partly because he proudly manufactured them and partly because they reminded him of his home country, Cuba.

His wife swarmed in with a freshly made cup of black coffee and happily set it on the small nesting table beside his chair.

"How sweet of you," he said, smiling amiably at her. She smiled back, but didn't say anything, leaving the room quietly. He took the whole coffee fast as was his custom and after the final sip, choked hard on the black liquid. His eyes popped open in fear and terror, and he fell forward onto his knees, holding his throat as he gasped his last breath.

"What have you done to me?!"

6

THE VISITATION

Beneath the slow-spinning ceiling fan in their baby-blue bedroom, John tossed and turned on top of their navy Ralph Lauren sheets. Finally dosing off, he dreamed of a black being about 5 feet 11 inches tall with no physical features other than an outline of a body. It climbed malevolently through the computer screen in his home office and swiftly cantered over to his bedroom straight to his side, where it began to strangle him with its gnarly black hands, using all its might. Awakening stricken with absolute spine-curdling terror, John's windpipe was so constricted that he lunged forward, gasping for air.

He woke Angela, hugged her tightly and shared with her what had happened. She couldn't believe it. The house wasn't haunted, she insisted. Couldn't be, they had only moved in a few months ago. He said he hoped not and lay back down, relaxing his back muscles. The severe throat constriction subsided after a minute, but John still had a catch in his throat that wouldn't go away. He lay awake terrified for hours and finally dosed off after watching that day's nightly news on YouTube on his iPad.

When John awoke, his throat was still slightly constricted and he could hear Howlin' Wolf barking in the kitchen. When he walked in, he was immediately struck dumbfounded at the sight of all six of the breakfast table chairs flipped upside down, resting on the edge of the kitchen table, and the barstools set right side up on top of the island. John took a step back, his jaw dropping to the floor in amazement. Then, he rushed out of the room to Angela and shook her violently.

"Get up angel! Get up! You just have to see this!" he exclaimed.

"What is it, you buffoon?"

"Come see, I swear...you won't believe it!" He shook her.

"Okay, I guess." She yawned and stood up slowly, moseying into the kitchen behind him.

"Oh...my...goodness, just who put the chairs on the table John?"

"I don't know love, but I am getting the hell out of here!" John ran back into the bedroom.

Angela followed. "Why? You think it's a ghost or something? Chairs just don't jump up onto tables babe."

"Well, they do now. We have a poltergeist or something."

"Okay, okay babe, I guess so, but what do you want to do?"

"I don't know, maybe we should go visit that Voodoo Queen on Duval Street. You know the one." John tossed on a red shirt on as he walked out of the closet.

"Her? I guess so, let's go. Let me throw some clothes on also and get to it."

7

MAGGIE AND HANK

M aggie May applied her red lipstick again, and then picked up her Louis Vuitton duffel bag off the luggage turnstile at the Key West International Airport baggage claim. Fortunately, she still had all her fashionable clothes and bags from her days as a model and she still looked good. Only now she wore King Solomon's Seal dangling from her necklace and a mood ring on her finger. Solomon's Seal apparently bore the wisdom of the ancient king.

A lame guy with disheveled black hair and a bushy moustache noticed her beautiful sculpted body and model features and came up to her, asking if he could help. She replied sure and let him walk her bag to the Uber waiting line. His eyes couldn't leave her face.

"So, what are you doing in Key West?" the guy, whose name was Scott, asked.

"Just here to see an old guy friend."

"Oh cool, why don't I give you a ride to his house then, I'd be happy to help."

"Okay, thanks."

"Let me take your bags," he offered, and picked up the

Vuitton duffle and they walked to his car. He stopped by an old
bronze rusted 1985 Cadillac Seville, unlocked the door and
proceeded to toss the duffel in the trunk. Maggie May eagerly
plopped down in the torn leather passenger seat, ripped from
years of use and the Florida sun, and checked her appearance
in the mirror again.

Scott drove Maggie to Duval Street and on to Truman
through the maze of Fantasy Fest traffic. Fantasy Fest, the
famous Key West Halloween-themed festival, lasts from
October 21st through the 31st.

They pulled up at a historic white clapboard cottage with a
white picketed fence, and she danced out. Scott begged her to
come stay with him at his house, but she insisted on being left
there. Standing on Hank's porch with her Louis Vuitton duffel,
she laughed when she saw the pair of skull votives fit for a
candle. Beside them sat two enormous pumpkins. She knocked
on the door. After four raps, no one answered, and she remem-
bered Hank had said he would leave a key under the "Welcome
Home" mat.

Maggie checked under the mat and sure enough the brass
key was there. She turned the key into the lock, it clicked open
and she pushed the creaking door forward. The house smelled
musty as some old houses do. She dropped her Louis Vuitton
duffle by the staircase and made her way to the kitchen, where
she swung open the enormous Sub-Zero refrigerator.

Hank was a gourmet foodie, mainly stocking healthy, fresh
food. Maggie skipped over the range of fruits piled on the
shelves and managed to find a bottle of Redi Whip whipping
cream, which she sucked down fast. She might have loved the
supernatural, but she was no granola when it came to her food.

She slammed the fridge shut and rummaged through the
pantry, where she found Hank's super-sized bag of Lays potato
chips. She tore the bag open and headed to the living room,

plopped down on the comfy sofa, flipped the TV on to *Ghost Hunters* and began stuffing the chips into her mouth.

Inspired by the show, she pulled her dowsing rods out of her duffle – two metal divination rods that she used to test earth vibrations and receive answers from spirits that had passed on – and sat on the floor Indian-style.

She started the process she always went through. She held the two small poles in her hand, while the two other short poles stuck forward at a 90-degree angle. Then Maggie asked a question, if the answer was yes, the poles would move towards the center coming close to each other, if the answer was no, they would spread apart. She knew Key West had a haunted history and was eager to test the waters. She asked the rods if there were any spirits that had passed on in Hank's house, but they moved apart. "Shucks," she said. "It isn't working. It should be a resounding yes on this Island of Bones."

At that moment, her old boyfriend Gusto from Paris texted her and she wrote back quickly, telling him all about how she was in haunted Key West, staying with her old buddy Hank. He asked when she was coming to Paris to watch another one of his fashion shows, and she said she didn't know, but maybe soon. Gusto implied he missed her so much since they had broken up. It flattered her, but she didn't reply.

Since her modeling days, she had always loved not replying to text messages in the middle of a conversation with a guy who liked her. She knew all the tricks and games. Stuff like that drove men crazy – and what did she care? She was a psychic goddess now. A female warrior.

At that moment, the door opened and in walked Hank.

"Hey babe," she said, jumping up and kissing him on the cheek. The memory of her old fling with Gusto melted away in an instant.

Hank was chewing gum, his black maverick hair slicked

back, his dimples pronounced by a smile full of white teeth. Still a stud, she thought.

"So, how's Vermont?" Hank followed her long, lanky body as she returned to the sofa.

"Good."

"Awesome. You know it's just me and my eight-toed Hemingway cat, Larry here. Don't know where the little fellow is, must be outside."

"Oh, I love cats, sometimes I feel like that's my spirit animal you know," she said, making a tiger claw in the air.

"Cool, he's a polydactyl with eight toes and one eye. Lost his eye to one of those wild Key West birds in the street last year, probably to a cockfight rooster who was jail broke. Anyway, let's go get something to eat girl, you look hungry!"

"Okay sure! I am jonesing for some good Cuban food."

The two walked over to Duval Street from Hank's cottage and crawled Duval for a little before stopping at Bien, an old gas station that had been renovated, painted pink and converted into a Cuban restaurant. Hank ordered them two slow-roasted Cuban ham and pork sandwiches with jalepeños, onions and garlic mayonnaise on freshly baked Cuban bread, while they sat and talked about life.

"It's so good seeing you girl. Tell me, what have you been doing living up there in Vermont? Out of sight, out of mind."

"Just stuff," she said and sipped her iced tea. "Hey, give me your hands. I can read your palms."

Hank smiled and said, "Sure," placing his hands upright into hers. She started tracing the left one with her thumb.

"Oh wow babe, you have long fingers and palms, that's a sure sign you have water hands like me. Oh baby!" she said, pumping her fists in the air. "That means we are in tune with our psychic ability and emotions."

Hank laughed. "Sounds good to me, sometimes when I am

out there on the water fly fishing, I know what the fish are thinking, it's like we're one."

"Me too, I mean not when fishing, but like with our customers at the shop, I can tell what each one wants sometimes. It's amazing."

"Really, you go girl. So cool." He sipped his Red Stripe beer. Gazing into her beautiful blue eyes, he asked, "So what are you wearing for Fantasy Fest tomorrow?"

"Nothing, I guess."

"You could wear my cop outfit. You would look so hot in my peaked cap."

She giggled and waited a moment. "Okay, let's see, lover boy."

8

THE VOODOO QUEEN OF DUVAL STREET

W alking down the colorful Duval Street, John led Angela to the Voodoo shop, which sat smack dab in between the Key Lime Pie Company and Outer Reef Fly-Fishing shop. The two lovers had visited both spots many times in the past two months since arriving, so John knew where to find Miss Anne, Key West's own Voodoo Queen. Crunched in between the two island staples, the tiny white store-front had her name hand-painted in gold leaf cursive on the broad bay window: *Miss Anne, The Voodoo Queen of Duval Street.*

The two entered, a bell chiming as they walked in.

Miss Anne was sitting in a highbacked rattan chair staring right at them, as though she knew they were coming. An older black woman in her sixties, her grey hair was wrapped up curiously in a bright dazzling yellow sash with red floral prints on it. She wore no earrings and her bone structure looked identical to Marie Laveau, the famous Louisiana Creole Voodoo princess. John had seen a portrait of Laveau on a trip to New Orleans when Angela and he had stopped into a Voodoo shop off the quarter.

"Howdy," she said, watching them.

"Hey there," John said, sitting down in front of the Queen. "How much is it to help us out with an issue?"

"Fifty dollars."

"How much time does that buy us?" John asked.

"As a matter of fact, time doesn't matter."

Intrigued, but still a little apprehensive, Angela sat down in the chair next to John.

"You two have come in peace, but you have found war."

"Yes, our house was assaulted this morning, by...by...ghosts! What else could it be?!" Angela squealed.

John banged his fist against the table. "Damn fools!"

"John, they are spirits, not people, for goodness sake," Angela said.

"I don't care, I want a word with them! I want answers."

"Calm down my son, Miss Anne has some tricks for you that will make everything go away."

"Aww hell, what is it? What have you got? Show us please," John asked.

"First of all, tell Miss Anne, what color is the haunted room?" Anne clasped her hands in front of her.

"Blue," Angela answered.

Miss Anne laughed a howling cackle. "Your ghost likes that color too. It is his favorite color. Why don't you paint the room...white?"

"But it's been blue for the last three months and we have had no problem."

"I don't care, it's a problem now."

"Last night, I had a nightmare about some...some...being! A black being vibrating with hate, coming to strangle me! And I wake up this morning and all the chairs in the kitchen are on the table!"

Miss Anne smiled. "Ahh, a shadow being. Let me do something." She reached over on her desk, picked up a stack of Tarot cards and began shuffling them, between her café-au-lait-colored fingers, each one adorned with gold rings.

"What, are we going to play some cards now?" John barked, frustrated.

"Seeing is believing, my son. But I am only reading for one of you. For both, you have to pay another fifty."

"Read for John, he has more problems than me."

"She's right. The ghost is probably attacking me. Besides I am the one who had the nightmare."

"Okay, Big John." She put the first card down face up. A bright red angry muscle-bound demon with horns stared up at them, holding his pitchfork in revenge.

"Wait. How do you know my name?"

"Yeah, that's so amazing Miss Anne!" Angela added.

"I know many things that you wouldn't believe my friends. Let's focus on the cards. They see more than me."

"Okay, whatever, tell us," John asked.

"The Devil. This card represents your past and being seduced by the physical world of pleasures."

"What is it about my past?" John said, squirming in his chair now.

"Not sure. That's for me to know and you to find out."

"Okay, I guess. Tell me something good please, flip the next card over."

"Okay, have it your way." She flipped the second card over.

"Aha, the Moon card. This is you now. It means something in your life is not what it seems. You are being dishonest with yourself about something."

"I am not sure what." John paused to think. Then he tapped his index finger on the table. "Show me another please."

The Voodoo Queen flipped the third card out.

"The Temperance card. It represents and pertains to your future. You need balance my son. That is all. Otherwise it could end badly with these ghosts, your past and the dreams."

"John," interjected Angela, "what she is saying is you need to stop your bad habits. Isn't that what the cards are saying?"

The Queen leaned back and looked at John. "Yes, stop your habits. The cigar makes you wheeze now. Your throat is tight from smoking. And this coffee you drink all day long to write." She shook her finger at him back and forth. "What's that really for? I mean, you can't handle this stuff you know. Many can, but not you. Big John is so nervous all the time from this stuff. It's the real Voodoo on you."

"Aw shucks, first the fortune teller asked me to stop eating this and start eating that back home, and now this!"

"Listen to her John, she knows what she is talking about," urged Angela. "Besides, I can't stand the smell of those cigars anyway. You know how clean Thai people are."

"What about my past? And the ghost? What does he mean in all this?"

"Your past is coming back around you somehow." The Queen paused. "Yes, this Dexter fellow, the crippled billionaire you cured, he will haunt you here."

"Dexter Wade? *What?* I mean, really?" John asked.

"Yes, listen, don't worry, things have a way of working themselves out when we are on the right path. I told you to paint the rooms in your house white. Move out for a week or so. When you come back, spread red brick dust on the front steps of your house to keep the evil spirits away. This will hex-proof your home. And one more thing... you must find a King Solomon Seal necklace to send these ghosts back to their graves once and for all."

"Okay, a King Solomon's Seal necklace. We will just pick one up tonight at the Wal-Mart. And some red brick dust, we can get that just about anywhere, right?" John quipped sarcastically.

Anne smiled. "Up to you, John. You can take what I say or you can leave it. But Miss Anne's sight don't lie." The words were hauntingly similar to his old friend Madame Bernadette's – she had said those very words about his weight loss.

"Shut up John." Angela frogged him on the arm. "Thank you so much Miss Anne!"

"You're welcome sweetie."

Angela pulled out fifty dollars from her pink Kate Spade wallet and paid Miss Anne.

"Thanks!" John said. "We will do all this stuff. Even if it takes a lot of work to find it. Hopefully, it will work."

"Sure you will. Oh, and John," Miss Anne said as he was walking away. "Believe in your spirit guide."

John turned his head. "But my guide, the wolf, she...uh... she left." He had a hint of sadness in his voice, his eyes starting to water.

"She's not a wolf now, but a bird, the talking kind."

9

TEMPTATION

After leaving the Voodoo shop, John asked Angela if she wanted a slice of key lime pie. She replied of course and the two walked into the Key Lime Pie Company next door, which was bustling with all manner of colorful people, the only clothes on their bare bodies being the body paint from the Parade Tattoo Parlor.

The lime-green paint on the walls of the joint got John's appetite going right away. Salivating over the pies in the glass case, his hands were warm and tingling again. His throat was still constricted, so he could imagine the cold, delicious tart pie soothing it as it traveled down to his tummy.

"I suppose you can have a slice baby," Angela said, watching him.

"Sure, I mean, I'm not fat anymore." He turned to her with a serious look. "Hey, why don't we get a whole pie and take it with us?"

"Are you sure? You won't eat it all at once, will you?"

"No way! Not anymore."

"Can I help you?" a saucy brunette with big lips and a nose-ring asked John.

"Sure, we'll take a whole key lime pie to go," John replied.

"Okay, one moment." In a minute, she handed him a white box with a full key lime pie inside and the couple moved on down to the register. As John was checking out, he reluctantly ordered an iced latte to go.

"Make it a large," he added, "with an extra shot." Angela frowned as she watched and then ordered an iced lemonade with freshly squeezed lemons.

"Just one for the road babe," he said, smiling at her. She gritted her teeth.

"Okay babe, but remember what Anne said. Temperance in all things."

"I know, I know."

They paid and sat down at a small black metal bistro table in a little nook by the window. Angela opened a hotel app on her phone, but every hotel was booked solid due to Fantasy Fest. It seemed only one room remained at the Chelsea House Pool and Gardens.

"What about this one?" Angela showed the front of the hotel photo on her phone to John.

"Looks old and spooky," he joked, "book it." He opened the lid to the pie box and scooped a hefty portion into his mouth, drowning it with the latte.

Angela reserved a room at the hotel. Two men walked into the shop dressed in white Elvis jumpsuits, the kind from his Vegas days – one of the various humorous costumes sprinkling the downtown during the festival. A blonde painted like Superman walked in behind them, a red "S" painted over her exposed large breasts, the rest of her torso blue. John and Angela both poked fun at the costumes.

They exited the shop and headed down Duval Street, stopping at the Conch Shack where they each ordered some conch ceviche. When they finished it, they both dug into the pie, and

John ate more than his fill. After eating, they reluctantly agreed to return to their house.

As though they might wake the dead, they slowly crept into the house to pack a week's worth of clothes. Howlin' Wolf whimpered when he saw them, and a draft permeated the house. They agreed to take Howlin' to the doggy hotel for the time being. Besides, he didn't need to be tangling with the ghosts at night, even if they dared return to feed and walk him. John threw a box of Cohiba Habanos, his golden Beretta cigar clipper and a lighter into his military issue duffel without Angela seeing them. While packing, nothing else strange occurred other than the cold air and Howlin's fearful nature, but they were spooked just being back at 121 Caroline Street nonetheless.

The pair loaded their Defender and drove straight to the doggy hotel where they dropped Howlin' Wolf off, who cried when they left him. Then they headed to the Chelsea House Hotel and checked in at the front desk. Some painted ladies strutted by, who John watched aimlessly as they passed.

Angela hit him on the arm, "Baby!"

"I am sorry babe, it was an accident, but they are naked for goodness sakes."

"Yeah, right."

The old lady behind the counter with curly grey hair and caked-on make-up sported a clear visor, and spoke in an old smokey voice, "Yeah, it gets really wild down here this time of year. Never been to the Fest before?"

"No...uh, we are new to the island," John said.

"Well, welcome! How long you staying?"

"Until John finishes his book. We absolutely love the Keys!"

"Oh, you're a writer? Me too! I have been here my whole life. Hey big guy, you look familiar, have I seen you before?"

"Me? No way, I'm nobody."

"Oh, must be my imagination, I see people all the time you

know," she said, and swiped their credit card. Then she handed them a key with a large black 18 on a gold oval.

"You guys are in room 18." She pointed the way.

THE SUNBURST-COLORED room didn't feel haunted at all. In fact, it was nice, clean and newly renovated. They unpacked their bags into the dresser and relaxed on the bed. Laughing about running away from a ghost at their house and the crazy Voodoo princess while in the safe room, the two enjoyed some relief from the wildness of the day's events. When Angela stopped laughing, John leaned over and kissed her lips, causing her to smile.

"Hey, did you bring your swimming suit?" he asked.

"Yep, sure did! Let's go for a dip!"

"Okay, can we make love after?"

"Maybe," she teased him.

She hopped up laughing and started to change, while John called the highest-rated painter he could locate on Google business. Tony, the owner of Five Star Painting, answered with a thick Italian accent and after some square footage discussion, quoted John a fee for painting all the blue rooms white, which included John and Angela's bedroom, the kitchen and the guest bedroom. John figured what the hell, maybe Miss Anne knew a thing or two, and gave the painter his American Express. Tony advised that Pablo would be there the day after tomorrow and John told him there was a key under the front door welcome mat. The work would take only a day or so.

Now they just needed to figure out where to get that damn Seal of Solomon and the red brick dust – John had almost forgotten about them both.

Angela emerged from the bathroom wearing a black string bikini that rode high on her beautiful dark thighs. He threw on his Tommy Bahama shorts, removed his shirt to reveal his rock-hard chest and abs and the two headed out to the pool. He was still red from fishing the other day, but eager to soak up some more sun.

Since moving from the mountains of Big Sur, John had become a Southern beach bum at heart. He was a Bubba now – his favorite word for a Key West native. He doubted whether anyone would ever call him that, but he loved the island through and through. His California heart now beat wildly to the rhythm of the small funky town at the southernmost point of America.

At the pool, Angela bronzed her back, while John read a Key West collection of ghost stories. After a while, John could tell she was snoozing. Across the way, an overweight gentleman with a paper-white fedora, a white polo and seersucker shorts was sucking on a fat maduro cigar. He fired it up and the smoke trailed over to John, who couldn't resist the urge to creep into their room and sneak a Habano. He grabbed the Beretta clipper and lighter and headed out onto Truman Avenue where he sparked the cigar and puffed it slowly while cruising down the avenue.

In a little while he came upon the Key West Cuban Coffee House, extinguished the cigar and ordered a single bucci instead of his usual afternoon double dose, and he sipped the espresso slowly, savoring every drop.

At that moment, he felt inspired to write, and perhaps get past page 100 in his new book. The halt was driving him mad. However, he didn't have his laptop and where would he write anyway? The thought crossed his mind that he could walk over to Starbucks up the street, buy a notepad and a pen on the way and write there. Let Angela know he had a mad creative streak coming through and needed to channel it. Perhaps he could order a latte or two as the day waned on.

At that moment, he realized how bizarre his mentation was. Miss Anne had said John needed temperance in all things. Was she saying he had to quit all coffee? That would mean no more writing too, correct? I mean, how could anyone write without coffee, John pondered. He laughed at the thought and at that exact moment, passed in front of Mississippi playwright and author, Tennessee Williams's house. "What a beaut," he thought, admiring the property.

He kept walking until a yellow smiling sun sticker caught his eye in the window of the Moon Goddess. Thinking he might find this silly Seal of Solomon pendant, he ducked in to look around. The store had shelves full of incense, hand woven shoulder purses, glass pipes for smoking marijuana, baja pullovers made out of hemp, divination cards, books on fairies, dowsing rods and a whole slew of other goodies.

"Can I help you?" a short blonde hippie asked.

"Oh yes, I am looking for a King Solomon Seal necklace, something like that."

"Hmm, never heard of one of those. Sorry."

"Aw shucks, okay, thanks." He left and, worried that Angela would miss him, pivoted back to the hotel.

When he arrived at the pool, he found Angela reading a shelter magazine, tanning her awesome legs. She looked so cute, John thought, and smiled as he swaggered over. Immediately after he sat down on the lounger, Angela shot him a look of dismay, "Where did you go John?"

"Just to the bathroom angel...what?"

"John? I smell you, you smell like cigarettes!"

"It's a cigar baby, it's not bad. I don't even inhale them!"

"I am mad at you! You know I don't like that smell. Besides, what about Miss Anne? She said you must stop all these bad habits babe. The damn devil is around us with these ghosts."

"I am working on it love, it just takes time, I only had one shot of bucci just then, usually I have two at this time of day. I will quit tomorrow, I promise."

"But you said you would stop! That means now. Tomorrow

is too late." At that she turned away, got up, and wrapped her towel around her beautiful tanned waist. "I am mad at you now." Then she swished away back to the room.

John huffed. As he sat there shaking his head, he wondered why she was so mad over a silly cigar. He needed a drink, something to take the edge off. He texted her that he was going down to Tony's for a quick drink and would be back later. She replied "k" and he knew she was mad. "K" always meant mad. John was in even more trouble but he didn't fully grasp it.

Growing up in a city, he had always dreamed of being some fat cat when he got older, frequenting wood-paneled polo clubs dressed in wool tailored trousers with a robust application of aftershave, smoking long Churchill cigars with other men and drinking brown liquor out of expensive glasses while talking stock prices. He banged his fist down on the lounger at the idea of giving up all of that. It was his idea of manhood. He was having this drink come hell or high water.

He stood up and exited the courtyard area to the street where he made his way down the alley to Captain Tony's, his favorite bar in Key West.

BACK IN ROOM 18, Angela was upset with John and crying alone. Ever since his wolf had run away in Big Sur and the couple had arrived in the salty Keys, he had become an addict again. Not for bad food like before, but for strong coffee and cigars. Sure, they were legal stimulants, but for John there was more to it. He lived to smoke and suck down those buccis. He acted as though he couldn't live without them. And Angela was starting think they were replacing her.

10

BEDAZZLED

Monday, October 26th

Maggie and Hank were sitting on the leather sofa in his candlelit living room, listening to Steve Tyrell's version of Sinatra's "Bewitched, Bedazzled and Bewildered" and eating stove-popped popcorn drizzled with real butter.

Hank leaned in and kissed her, "I love you babe."

"I love you back," she said, and they Frenched for a while. She took her top off, swung it around her head five times and threw it into the hall, then straddled him.

She held her finger up revealing her violet-colored ring. "My mood ring has turned violet, you big stud. You know what that means?"

"No babe, no idea."

"It means I am very excited."

"Oh yeah, me too."

They both laughed and stripped off their clothes and began making love to each other on the couch.

When they finished, Hank was holding Maggie and noticed her necklace was missing.

"Hey babe, what happened to your necklace?"

"My what?" She touched her neckline. "Oh, my goodness, King Solomon's Seal! I must have lost it."

"Where did you lose it?"

"Not sure, it must have fallen off while we were strolling on Duval after lunch. The clasp has always been loose. No worries, I'll get another one."

"What does it mean anyway?"

"It's just for protection and good measure. King Solomon was one of the wisest and wealthiest kings to ever live."

"Yeah, I remember him from studying the Bible when I was younger. Let's try to find it tomorrow."

"Okay," she said, and got up, exposing her scorching lean body. "Wait one minute." She walked over to her Louis Vuitton in the other room, pulled out a nurse's outfit she had packed for Fantasy Fest, put it on and strutted back in.

"Saucy," he said. Then she straddled him again and the song "Witchcraft" came on from her playlist. Larry, Hank's one-eyed eight-toed cat, pranced over and sat down beside them on the sofa.

Larry caught Hank's eye and he was taken back. "Oh my, ole Larr has something crazy in his mouth baby. Look!" Turning Maggie saw that indeed there seemed to be something green protruding from Larry's mouth.

"Eww, yuck, what is it?" she cried, and stood up.

"It looks like a racoon paw," Hank said as he leaned forward. Meanwhile, Larry just stood there. Hank started tugging on the paw, but Larry wouldn't drop it.

"Eww, don't touch it!" Maggie said.

Hank gave it a good tug and the hand finally snapped out of Larry's mouth. Examining the greenish petrified looking paw, Hank said, "It's definitely some kind of animal hand."

"Oh, gross Hank."

"Hey maybe it's one of those chupacabras! You know they got 'em down in Puerto Rico."

Maggie laughed. "Now you're talking my language. Let's take a look I guess." She came over and the two studied it together. Agreeing it wasn't from this world, they finally tossed it outside into the neighbor's yard and started wrestling again on the couch. Larry came back over, this time with no paw in his mouth.

"I think ole Larr might bite your one-eyed willy," she joked.

"Oh no, Larry, get down, get down boy! Don't bite me." They both laughed and fell into each other's arms, kissing.

11

MILLER

B ig John sipped his Pabst Blue Ribbon beer slowly at Captain Tony's. Bras of every size and color were tacked to the ceiling and license plates of varying colors from all over America adorned the walls.

Tony's was the oldest watering hole in Key West. Established in 1851 as an icehouse and morgue, it was a Key West legend and home to a slew of ghost stories. The infamous hanging tree grew out of the ground in the middle of the bar. On that tree, sixteen pirates and one deranged murderous woman swung by the neck to their deaths. Legend has it that woman, known as the Lady in Blue, still haunts the place.

The song "Brokedown Palace" by the Grateful Dead was playing through the speakers and John laughed because it was one of his favorite songs. He thought about the name of Angela, and of his favorite band, The Grateful Dead, and it seemed quite bizarre considering their situation with the ghost and all. I mean, I wonder if that ghost was grateful to be dead, John thought. Guess not.

A very old man with stark white hair and a Hemingway

build was sitting beside John. The two had been sharing the silence for a minute or so until the old man spoke quietly.

"Name is Miller." The man gazed at John without extending a hand.

"John."

"That's a common name. Common and boring," the old-timer said, before draining his Montgomery Martini and sliding the glass over to a line of previously battled glasses.

"Order me another, friend, and make it cold and icy," Miller said.

"Okay," John said and watched him, waiting for the bartender. The bar was dark, but he swore the man looked like the spitting image of Mr. Hemingway, perhaps a little older.

"I come here once a week or so to get out of the house. I like to drink at home usually with my six-toed cats. Most nights we box, me and Shine and the boys, but tonight, I am alone. This place used to be old Sloppy Joe Russell's, loved it back then."

"I hear ya," John said. "Are you a native?"

"No, came here in twenty-eight. Been here ever since."

"Twenty-eight...sir, that would make you over a hundred unless you came here when you were nine years old. And I swear you ain't that old mister," John insisted, smiling.

"Been here ever since I said!" Miller said. "What are you about?" The old man stared at John. He looked like a sailor and John could tell he had spent a lot of time on a boat in the sun out at sea.

"Nothing I guess, I mean I am just me."

"Aww hell, you gotta choose your battles son, nothing gets done unless you fight. Look at me, I am here fighting like you. Even drinking is a battle and writing too. The sun also rises!"

Some fraternity boys in starched polo button-ups and short khaki beefy leg shorts approached wearing those tan leather flip flops popular with college kids and crowded around John to place orders for their beers. John took his drink and got up. When he turned to say goodbye to Miller, the man had vanished. Just like that. John looked around. "Hey man, did you see the guy that was sitting here?" he asked the bartender.

"What guy?" the bartender replied, confused.

12

DEXTER'S BACK

Earlier that day in Palo Alto, Techtonic billionaire Dexter Wade was drunk, reclining in his custom black and white cowhide-covered chair. Recently diagnosed with Lou Gehrig's Disease, he had been given only two years to live by his doctor and was in constant pain.

From the day he walked out of the doctor's office, in every way he knew how, he had reached out to Big John Hoover, the miracle boy who cured him of his paralysis many years ago, but John never replied.

In spite of respiratory complications from the disease, he had taken a convoy to Big Sur where he heard the mystery boy was living with his wife. After slipping hundred-dollar bill after hundred to shop and inn keepers asking after John's address, he found the cabin where John and Angela used to live, but no one was there. All the furniture was missing and a For Sale sign was staked by the entrance to the land.

Finally, Dexter managed to strong-arm the real estate agent selling the land into revealing John's phone number and where the couple had gone. Dex was able to reach John by phone in Key West.

John reluctantly agreed to treat the crazy billionaire. The two met on a Skype call the next day at three pm, but John's magic hands didn't work like they sometimes did. Furious, Dexter tipped his office desk over, cursing John, even though John explained it sometimes happened.

That night, Dexter bought a special Day of the Dead edition of high-priced tequila that came in a clear skull bottle and drank it fast and hard in a state of misery. He couldn't taste a cigar anymore due to how bad his lungs were, but he could taste revenge, and was going to send Big John to his grave one way or another.

13

GHOST #2

B ack at the hotel, John entered to find Angela sleeping soundly in her navy silk pajamas. He crept into bed and whispered "I love you" in her ear. She woke and cringed at the sight of him. "Move away from me! Go sleep on the couch John. I am mad at you buddy."

"Aw shucks," he said and took his pillow over to the cramped sofa with no blanket. It was nine pm, so John popped his Apple laptop open, bringing up his book, *Healing Hands*. He scrolled to page 100 where he had left off, but nothing came. Even the booze he had at Tony's wasn't greasing the writing wheels. Neither was he sleepy. He was really jonesing for another Habano but felt guilty even at the thought of them.

Angela and he loved dance, so he searched for some concerts. That would cheer her up, he thought. As he scrolled through the island events, he saw a *The Hip Abduction* concert, one of his favorite new Florida-based bands. The show was general admission at Hog's Breath Saloon on Duval, so he bought two tickets and closed his laptop.

At that moment, the visage of an elderly man wearing stately clothes from another era stood in the doorway of the bathroom, staring at him with a cool eye. In the man's right hand was a cigar. The room smelled strong like the tobacco too, but also slightly sweet like aromatic honey. It was now as cold as death. John's throat became extremely tight. So tight he could barely suck a breath through his disappearing windpipe. He shook Angela with all his might and she again woke startled, demanding to know what it was.

"Look, look! There's a bloody ghost in our room!" He pointed to the bathroom doorway.

Angela looked up, but the man was gone. She did however observe the smell of strong cigars and the temperature.

"John, I don't see it, but did you smoke in here?" Her face awash in disbelief.

"No way, it was the ghost, baby, I swear. He had a damn cigar. I am not smoking anymore ever again. Makes you too mad and my throat is so tight now from them anyway."

"Oh gosh, a ghost again, really? Like our house?"

"Yes baby, I swear! You gotta believe me girl."

"It is really cold in here. Oh no, I'm scared now John. Why don't you come back to bed and hold me?"

Relieved, John returned to the bed where he embraced Angela. And she dozed off again shortly after, but he barely slept a wink due to the ghost, and his throat was so tight he almost couldn't breathe.

As soon as the sun cracked through the windows on Sunday, October 27th, John woke with his throat a little better, but still bad, so he threw on some jean shorts, his yellow Tommy Bahama linen shirt and donned a panama estancia hat before waltzing to the front desk for answers. Today, the old lady was there again.

"Excuse me, is this place haunted? I saw a ghost in my room last night."

"Oh yeah, that," she said, sipping her coffee. John observed this woman always had coffee. Probably on her second one. He could only imagine with envy the milligrams of caffeine running through her veins now. If he was allowed to have coffee, perhaps he could figure out this whole mystery with the ghosts.

"What?" John asked.

"Well, you are in room 18 right?"

"Yeah, I guess. So what?"

"Well, everyone and their mother knows that's Mr. Delgado's room. He died there."

"So, please tell me, just who is this Mr. Delgado?"

"He used to own the joint. Yeah, he was a cigar baron back in the day, but his wife killed him, right there in your room." She slapped the desk and walked away to get another cup of coffee. John needed the juice also and just seeing the cup filled him with upset.

"What is this murder in our room? We can't stay there, move us, please!"

She filled her cup with the coffee and, moseying back over to John, looked him kindly in the eye, took a long slow sip, then said, "Most people get a kick out of it. He's a harmless ghost anyway."

"Well not us! We left our house and came here to escape a ghost, and now...this!"

She smiled, "Really, wow, well I can't help you bud, don't you know this island is haunted? Get used to it. Besides, it's the only room we got. You know, it's Fantasy Fest now."

"Okay, what should I do? Can we ghost-proof the place, maybe place a little red brick dust at the entrance? What?"

"Never heard of that, but you can try, I guess. Maid will probably just clean it up tomorrow though."

"I don't believe this," John said waving his arms in the air as he walked off.

Back at the room, Angela and he agreed to go out for some breakfast at Banana Café on Duval Street, one of their favorites.

They sat at the one of the best tables on the outside porch. After ordering some La Super crepes with egg, ham, sausage, swiss cheese and bechamel sauce, Angela sipped her coffee slowly while John watched enviously as he drank his orange juice, which didn't taste freshly squeezed – it was some ultra-pasteurized, always-from-concentrate crap. He was enduring some coffee withdrawal symptoms as well, a slight headache being one.

At that moment, a gigantic red and blue macaw parrot, the likes of which no man has ever seen, landed on the wall around the porch right next to the pair.

"Oh, look baby, it's a parrot, wonder if it might be my spirit animal!"

"Is this what Miss Anne was talking about babe? Look at how red it is. I have never seen a blue macaw like this."

"Me neither," John said, studying the bird in amazement.

The bird sat there for a moment, nodded at the two and then flew off into the heat. The two lovers wondered about what they had just seen, and John felt reborn, like his spirit was coming back to him after a long hiatus since his wolf had left.

The two talked and in spite of the mild headache from the coffee detox, John managed to grin at his sweet wife's beautiful face. When her crepes came, he spooned a bite and fed it to her. He couldn't help himself, and leaned forward to kiss her on the lips.

AFTER SITTING at Mallory Square on the water and drinking two pina coladas, the two lovers wandered over to American author Ernest Hemingway's historic house on 907 Whitehead Street, where John quickly learned the legendary writer's middle name was Miller, shooting an eerie chill straight up his spine. The salty dog had also come to Key West in 1928, the same year John's bar friend named Miller had migrated here.

He decided not to mention the event to Angela, the whole idea of having a drink with Hemingway's ghost was just too strange, and he had to keep her calm, as he sensed she was becoming unsettled after last night's events. After touring the grounds, the two made it to the Hog Breath Saloon on Duval Street for the show.

14

A GIFT FROM ABOVE

Hank had the next day off work, so he and Maggie decided it would be their day for Fantasy Fest. She skipped over the nurse's outfit she had packed, and Hank's sexy peaked police cap, to go as a psychic seer with turquoise eye liner and a blue robe. It wasn't sex on a stick, she said, but it made Hank hot anyway. He went as a football player for the Green Bay Packers, his shirt cut short to display his bronzed six-pack ab muscles.

By three pm, the two lovers were taking vodka shots with two gay bears at LaTeDa on Duval, talking about tank tops and jorts. An hour later, they were a little drunk down at Sloppy Joe's Bar singing karaoke songs in front of a rowdy crowd full of painted ladies and wild exotic costumes.

Hank launched into a full rendition of "Superstition" by Stevie Wonder, while Maggie waited her turn to sing Fleetwood Mac's "Black Magic Woman."

Afterwards, the pair hit up the Conch Shack for some iced Red Stripe beers and two orders of fried conch. The beers were so cold there were miniscule slivers of ice floating in the ale. Maggie told the server Sue that she had lost her King Solomon necklace there the other day and asked if she had seen it. Before Sue could answer, a brilliant red macaw flew by, dropping the necklace on top of Maggie. It landed in her lap. Stunned, she held it up.

"My necklace! I found it... or it found me!" The macaw perched on the roof of the Shack, studying her and Hank. "That bird baby, it helped us." She pointed at it.

"Holy hell, that was incredible babe. What a wingspan. Guess it was meant to be."

"Of, course it was. Everything is."

She put the necklace on and after finishing their meal, the two wandered down to the beach to relax and watch the sun set.

When it got dark, Maggie turned to Hank and said, "Hank, show me that famous Key West cemetery, I want to see where all the dead people live."

"Hahaha, alright babe, to the Key West Cemetery we shall go. It's spooky girl."

15

THE HIP ABDUCTION

A rriving an hour early, they managed to make it to the front for the show. There were no seats, just general admission. Almost the whole crowd was in costume for Fantasy Fest. A gay guy dressed in a silver Tin Man from *The Wizard of Oz* costume, a woman dressed like the Statue of Liberty, and another bare woman painted like a Louis Vuitton bag were just a few of the many outfits.

The five-man band came out and launched into the high tempo song "Come Alive" – John's favorite song.

"This group is the best thing since the Dead," Angela said, and John couldn't help but agree as they danced furiously. The two danced and danced. When the song, "Wandered Away" came on, a cool breeze blew over them, and the lovers slow danced, gazing deep into each other's eyes and for a moment, the ghosts in their new life were missing.

Angela was wearing a beige coastal looking shirt with stonewashed blue jean shorts, and her black hair was braided tight on both sides. They kissed to the wild music; this song always sounded like Africa to John, reminding him of the Kenyan desert winds on his trip there many years ago with his parents. A hippie couple beside them must have been tripping on magic mushrooms and the smell of dank marijuana was hanging like a fat cloud in the air, appearing as a mirage of fog.

When the song ended, John excused himself to the bathroom, leaving Angela to dance alone. After exiting the porta potty, which was yellow with the name of the company, Pot-O-Gold, stamped on the side, a man with Mexican Day of the Dead skeleton face-paint in black and white approached John, asking him if he could please help his wife who was sick from drinking too much.

"I know who you are," the man said, "you're that healer, right?"

Remembering his hands, John agreed, and followed the man reluctantly. It was duty.

The skeleton-face man, dressed in all black, led him down a narrow alley where a college-aged brunette woman was laying on the ground in distress. John leaned down to her to help, and as he did, the man in skeleton face shot him with a needle in the neck from behind. John fell over in a state of blackout.

AWAKE SUDDENLY IN A DARK, musty place, something mysterious crawled up John's shirt. He could feel it moving along the length of his chest. Slowly, it moved up his neck and near his face. His breath was shallow from the lack of oxygen in the tight space, and his throat was still quite constricted from all the juju surrounding him. He struggled to move his arms much because the container he was in confined them. His fingers combed over the bottom of it, which was rock solid like stone. He was trapped in a stone catacomb.

The insect, which John concluded by its many legs must be a spider, reached his neck and slowly crept forward, over his chin and up near his lips. At his mouth it stopped, and John wiggled in panic. He decided to blow his breath as hard as he could in spite of the constriction in his throat. The blast thrusted the spider off his mouth, and it bounced off his chest and landed on the bottom of the vessel. John yelled at the top of his lungs for help.

BACK AT THE CONCERT, Angela became increasingly worried about her husband and kept texting and calling him, but his phone went straight to voicemail. Finally, she went to security seeking help. The event gave her déjà vu of the time many years ago in Big Sur when John was kidnapped by that thug billionaire Dexter. Miss Anne had said Dexter was around them again. The security team assured Angela that John was probably just hanging out with some friends or lost somewhere in the crowd. She insisted he didn't know anybody because they had just recently moved to the island. She walked off, bawling her eyes out. She kept texting John, but no reply came.

JOHN MANAGED to grab his lighter from his pocket and spark it. Sure enough, he was locked in a stone deathbed. He pushed on the roof of the casket, but it didn't budge one bit. After calling for help over and over again until his voice gave no more, he nodded off in a sleep.

A little while later, the top of the vessel moving woke Big John. Startled, he looked up only to see a phantom frail bald man with thin round glasses, a white beard, sporting a crisp white button-up shirt and a black bow tie staring back at him.

John was so startled that he screamed. He had actually seen the very man on a Key West themed episode of the TV show *Ghost Hunters* and knew it was none other than Count Carl Tanzler von Cosel and that he must be coming for Elena "Helen" Milagro de Hoyos, the corpse the Count had stolen many years ago and taken to his house to live with when he was living on the island as a radiologist. John must have been placed in her very casket. Terrified, John bolted up and the ghost circled around the room howling, *Where is she? Where is she? Where is my wife?*

"I don't know, I don't know," John did his best to have a dialog with the phantom.

Skulls were scattered all over the mausoleum's floor, probably a hack by whoever put him there to ward off visitors. Seeing them, John climbed out of the tomb and picked up a big femur bone and swatted at the phantom, but the ghost just moved through it like the wind. Furious, John ran out of the tomb into the above-ground cemetery that spanned hundreds of feet in both directions.

Making his way down the alleys of tombstones, he sensed all the spirits' eyes on him. I need to get out of here, he thought. It's the living dead here now. The gates of hell must be wide open.

Seeing the black iron-gated entrance to the cemetery up ahead, John gunned for it, but when he reached it, sure enough, it was locked.

Everything surged back through his mind. Angela, the concert and the needle in his neck. Who had done that and why? Was it Dexter? It didn't make sense. He had no enemies – he was Big John, the healer. He was in a living nightmare now. He prayed to God that he would give up all his vices if He would only carry him out of this crazy mess. His thoughts turned to his wife. What was she doing? He had to telephone her. He looked at his phone, but the battery was dead. Then, the giant macaw from lunch landed on top of the iron fence, where it studied his face. The bird wanted to help, but what could she do? He was a stranger in a strange land. So, he banged on the fence for what felt like an eternity, while the bird watched and waited. Exhausted, John collapsed in a slumber.

. . .

ARRIVING at the cemetery for Maggie, Hank was cruising past the front gate when they saw the beautiful macaw from the Conch Shack perched on top of the iron fence. Hank stopped to point the bird out to Maggie when they both saw John's back slumped against the iron poles.

"Oh crap, some freeloader got drunk in the cemetery again. Wait one minute babe."

"Sure, can I come? I just love waking the dead."

"Hahaha, no you wait here. I don't want to disturb him too much."

Unlocking the gate with a key Hank had been given a long time ago for patrolling the place, he lit his flashlight in John's eyes. John woke, shielding the light with his right forearm.

"Hey buddy, what are you doing here?" Hank asked.

"Nothing, just resting, someone...they...they, well they put me in that tomb over there." John pointed towards Elena's tomb. "And I...couldn't...couldn't get out."

"Tomb? What? Sounds like you've been doing the Duval crawl all night buddy. Stand up for me."

Hank helped John up. Then he asked John to turn around, before patting him down.

"You know sleeping here drunk is enough to take you in." Hank gently pulled John's arm back behind his back and cuffed him, read him his rights, then he led him into the squad car where the blue lights still spun around, flashing color into the night.

Maggie immediately recognized John through the squad car window. When he entered the back, she asked, "John, is that you?"

"Oh yeah, who's asking?" John looked up, still dazed from the shot.

"It's me, Miss Maggie May from Santa Monica High! You remember me John, come on!"

"What? Oh my," he said confused. "What on earth are you

doing here?" He leaned forward to get a good look at her as she was turned his way.

"I am just in town a few days vising Hank. I live in Vermont now where I work at a psychic shop."

Hank got in and overheard the two talking.

"Cool, well yeah Angela and me just moved here from Big Sur for me to write a book. I just had to get out of that cold California weather. It was killing us."

"I know what you mean, Burlington is freezing most of the year."

"Wait, you two know each other?" Hank asked.

Maggie laughed, "Yeah Hank, this is Big John! Remember him? The guy who cured that crippled boy."

Hank studied John's face in the mirror. "Oh yeah, you do look familiar big guy. How's it hanging man?"

"Alright I guess, hey look, are you going to let me go or what?"

Hank thought for a moment. "Rather not, you were just too spooked back there."

"Shoot. Okay whatever." John paused. "So, what were you guys doing at the cemetery anyway Maggie?"

"Well, I just really wanted to see the cemetery, I love ghosts now. We went to Fantasy Fest earlier today and found my Solomon necklace at the Conch Shack where it fell off the other day. Sounds stupid I know, but..."

"Wait, did you say your Solomon necklace? *Like King Solomon's Seal?*"

"Yeah, so what? You can have it." She touched it with her fingers, looking at it for a moment. "It's nothing to me. Some old guy came into the shop one day in Applebury and gave it to me, said it would bring me good luck or something."

"My goodness, I need that necklace. It will send all these ghosts that have been haunting my wife and me back to their graves for good."

"Really? Wow, well, sure." She removed it and managed to hand it through the police grating separating the front and back seats.

"Oh, my goodness." John sat back flabbergasted, clenching it in his hand. "I found it! Get me home!"

On the way to the station, John explained what happened at the concert and about the ghost in the tomb, and Hank believed him but said that he still had to take him downtown for his own safety.

At the station, John thanked Maggie and gave her his phone number, so the couples might meet up for a beer. Hank said he would do his best to get him discharged quickly.

Then, John was booked and led to a holding cell full of strange characters and a few Fantasy Fest drunkards. He was told to wait on his customary phone call until his papers were processed. Fortunately, no one recognized him inside as the cure guy. A slender black guy with a goatee kept singing like a broken record, "Key West, come on vacation, leave on probation." Everyone asked John what he got busted for, and he didn't really know what to say because he hadn't done anything wrong. Believing in ghosts, he thought, but didn't say a word.

His Bahama shirt wasn't helping anything though: he looked rich, and the inmates called him Opie after the redheaded boy Opie Taylor from the 1960s *Andy Griffith Show*, even though he had never felt like a nerd before and his hair wasn't even red.

After talking with Hank, Maggie arranged to have John released quickly. Finally, John was allowed to call Angela. Panic-stricken, she received the call from John, leaning up in the hotel bed, distraught.

"John? Tell me where you have been! I have been worried sick."

"Yeah, I'm at the police station babe. Some guy in a skull and bones costume led me over to his sick wife and right when

I reached her, he stuck a needle in my neck. Next thing I know, I wake up in a damn coffin in the Key West Cemetery and there is a ghost howling around the mausoleum's walls. Then, old Maggie May, that crazy girl from my high school, picked me up with this cop dude I used to know as well. This stuff is crazy baby! I mean you can't make it up!"

"What did you say?"

"You heard it, I am telling you, it's the truth. It's so weird."

"Oh, my John, you really are telling me the truth. I can hear it in your voice. Well after that scare at our house, I would believe anything."

"Wait, there's more, Maggie has the Solomon necklace."

"You're kidding me!"

"No! And guess what? She gave it to me! I'll tell you more when you pick me up."

"Really? Wow, great I am on my way."

Angela picked him up in the Defender crying and John told her all about Maggie's necklace. The two agreed to return to Miss Anne the next day. Surely, she would have answers about this fiasco, his throat and the graveyard.

16

THE BEACH

Monday, October 28th

The next day, Hank left for work at nine am, while Maggie slept in. She woke at noon and took a long, hot shower. Slipping on her peach-colored string bikini and a white girly beach coverup, she grabbed her canvas tote bag that had her initials stitched in hot pink on the side, filled it with some essentials and her dowsing rods and headed out to the curb where she requested an Uber.

Whatever she wore, she looked great in, even if it was ragged blue jeans or old wrinkled clothes. Her beauty was remarkable. Sure, she had been beautiful in high school, but she really transformed into an exceptional vision as she got older. Even on her worst hair days, guys asked for her number. It was ironic really because now she worked for a palm reader and believed there was more to life than appearances.

The Uber dropped her at the Southernmost House Hotel around three pm and she bought a straw beach hat at the hotel lobby, then wandered over to the beachside bar where she ordered a French Kiss drink, applied some more lipstick while looking in her pocket mirror and waited for Hank to get off work. She wondered about John. What he was doing here? And what on earth was that strange night at the cemetery? How could he be here, of all people? She no longer was interested in him at all and he hardly recognized her. She had moved on years ago but was still curious. Maybe the three could meet up and have a few drinks and talk about life and spirits.

17

ROUND TWO WITH MISS ANNE

"I see my children have come back to me," Miss Anne said. "How's it goin' my babies?"

John sat down in a quick motion while Angela was too nervous to sit. "Oh Miss Anne, this town is crazy! Last night, someone stuffed me in a coffin after some skeleton-face guy needled me in the neck at a concert."

"I see," she said, unassuming. All the candles on her altar were torched in a fiery glow and the hurricane lamps with their different colored liquids were lit on her table today. "Do you have the necklace yet my son?"

"Yes," he said, lifting it off his chest where it dangled to show her.

"Good man. Now, let's look at your cards. I am going to lay them down right now." She shuffled the stacked deck and then said, "You only get one card today for it represents your past, present and future now." Then she flipped over one single card. "My oh my, it's the Joker."

"Okay, well, come on, tell us, what does it mean?" John begged.

"Someone is tricking you Big John. I already told you the

Devil card represented your past. Well someone from your past is around you playing tricks. Sometimes, the Joker tarot represents the comedian or court jester, but not today, this one follows the Devil, who is a great trickster. Be very careful. There is danger at every turn for you now."

"Maybe it's that Dexter guy," John said. "What do you think Angela?"

"Yeah, maybe so. But what can we do, should we go home? Even the inn we are at is haunted!"

Miss Anne laughed. "What inn?"

"The Chelsea House," Angela answered.

"Oh, my, no, not there, that place is like a voodoo playhouse. Genies everywhere there. Have been ever since Mr. Delgado was murdered."

"We know, we know," John said. "But what can we do?"

"Well someone wants you dead. Have you stopped smoking yet?"

"Oh yeah and between that and the necklace, my throat feels a lot better now."

"Good, put the red brick dust at your house, that should help protect you from the Joker for now. Do that and we'll see."

John paid Miss Anne with a crisp fifty plus another fifty-dollar tip for her help. Then the two walked out into the street.

18

THE GETAWAY

Back on the beach, Maggie May was laying in a plastic lounge chair, oiling her long legs with a dark bronzing oil, thinking about Hank and how cool he was compared to all the Vermont preppies she had dated.

Sitting there, she pulled out her dowsing rods and started to detect for ghosts. She had caught the attention of just about every guy on the beach and now even more so with her strange rods. This time while dowsing she received a yes, that there was a ghost nearby in the Southernmost Hotel. She decided she would wander over and try to find it after tanning her body. She began reading a dream interpretation book when a young lifeguard with ripped abs and a head full of dirty blonde hair cruised over.

"Mind if I help," the young guy said, "name is Frank."

From the street, Hank approached and asked, "What are you doing there, bozo?"

The young guy turned his head and said, "Hey back off bud!"

"No way, dude, I saw her first," Hank said, smiling. He

walked up and sat down on Maggie's chair. The guy wandered away, shaking his curly head.

"I thought you would never come," she said, a mouth full of big funny teeth.

"Well you thought wrong, Hank is here, what do you need babe? Legs or back first?"

"Start with my legs." She pushed a painted white toe forward towards him. "How cute are my toes?"

"Cuter than mine," he hollered. "I look like a wild animal down there."

"Well what do you want to do stud?"

"I don't know, reminisce, go back to my place and tangle up like two wild bobcats going at it."

She made a playful tiger roar sound while mimicking a cat claw gesture with a feline face at him and they both laughed. "Okay, you know I am like a cat babe, but can I have one more drink here, I want to share a sunset with you," Maggie said.

"Sure babe, what you drinking? I'll get us some more."

"Some White Claw lime on you."

"Anything for you, my bobcat babe."

Hank returned with the drinks. Sitting there watching the sun fall, he told Maggie how last night he had dreamed they were on a sailboat sailing towards an island in the distance.

"Really? No way!"

"Yeah, maybe we should do it babe! I will ask for my vacation time and we'll charter a sailboat to Bimini."

"Sounds perfect love. Then both our dreams will be coming true."

She texted John asking him if Angela and he wanted to meet up.

"Hey Maggie, thank you guys so much for your help last night, but probably not the best idea if we meet up given our past together, you know."

"Really? Oh no. Well okay, I get it."

19

CIGAR SMOKE

J ohn and Angela returned to the Chelsea Inn where they waited patiently in their room for the painters to finish at their house. John leaned his back against some pillows to read a rod and reel magazine, while Angela wandered off to go get a soda from the vending machine. Suddenly, the smell of cigar smoke rose throughout the whole room, filling it.

John sat there tongue-tied in amazement as he braced himself for the ghost of Mr. Delgado to appear and start moving furniture, but nothing happened.

In a minute, Angela opened the door, astonished by the smell.

"Oh boy, you are in a big trouble now." She glared at John, her fists on her hips.

"I didn't smoke in here, it's that damn cigar-smoking ghost baby that haunts this room. It just started stinking like cigars all of a sudden. I promise." Holding his hands up in surrender.

"John, again? Are you serious? Why doesn't he ever show himself to me?"

"Okay, I know, I know, it's weird. But what about that doll

that haunts Key West? What do they call him, Robert the Doll? That's kooky."

"Yes, yes, I know, so what? I am gonna believe you this time," she said jumping on the bed, "since you are so cute, and Miss Anne says this place is haunted. Plus, you've quit the cigars and coffee too you big stud!"

"Thanks babe. My throat feels a lot better since cutting the coffee and cigars, even after the ghost was just here! I can't believe it. It's easier to breathe now!"

"Really, wow!"

"Yeah, I don't get it, but who even cares about it. I am tired babe, all this craziness is just too much."

"I know love, let's make love."

"With the stupid ghost here and all?"

"Yeah, why not? It's not like the stupid guy cares." They both laughed and then kissed.

20

THE HAZY KEYS

Dexter Wade strutted into a vacant Miss Anne's Voodoo shop on Duval Street, sat down and slammed a wad of hundreds onto the old lady's desk, then he coughed and wiped the sweat off his brow.

"What do you want Dexter?" She leaned towards him.

"You know my name?"

"Yes, and I see you coming here for something you don't want to know about."

"I want to know where the boy is, the healer. Only he can save me."

She leaned back.

"Okay, have it your way. He lives at 121 Caroline Street, go there and find him tomorrow, but be good or else..." And the irises of her eyes turned green like a snake's, with black slivers in the center.

Frightened, he walked away and wandered the downtown with his friend Jason Streak. They started the night off at a strip club where they proceeded to get hammered on Mint Juleps served in ice-cold tin cups. Then after a round of the strip club nachos, they staggered around Duval where they bought a couple of Cohibas at one of the endless wooden open-air cigar stands.

"I really shouldn't do this," Dexter said, admiring the stoogie, "but what the hell. All those legs and that booze has me craving for one." He lit the stick up and handed the lighter to Jason, who lit his.

After the first drag, Dex tasted what he could only imagine was the venom of a cobra coming through the smoke from the cigar. Jason said his cigar tasted like tobacco. Furious, Dex demanded Jason take a puff of his.

"Tastes fine to me."

Dex swiped it from him and stomped it out with his black cowboy boot. "It's that lady we saw today. She's some kind of Voodoo witch. Put a spell on me with those evil eyes. Do you have the skeleton key for tomorrow?"

"Yeah, I got it man."

"Good, and it can open any lock like you say? You're sure?"

"Yeah, that's what the cop told me."

21

SANDY CORNISH

1866

S andy Cornish, a black freed slave, stood before a crowd of angry white onlookers in Port Leon, Florida, holding a long knife in his right hand.

Addressing the group sternly, he spoke, "I purchased my freedom, but my papers got burned in the fire and under no circumstances will I be held in bondage ever again to return to New Orleans."

Gasps and roars emerged from the grumbling crowd. At that moment, Sandy silenced them all by stabbing himself violently in the leg, creating a four-inch deep gash, then he drew the knife down ten inches. Blood streamed from the wound, running down his leg. Then, he cut the muscles on the ankle of the same leg and, in a finale of blood and gore, he chopped off one of the fingers on his left hand, and stuffed it in his mouth like a popsicle as blood ran down his face.

Considered worthless as a slave by the white folk there, covered in blood, and feeling quite faint, Sandy's friends put him in a wheelbarrow and carried him home where his wife tended to his wounds. He was destined to be a free man again.

22

BIMINI

B ack at Hank's house, Maggie and he rolled around on the sheets of his king-sized sleigh bed, making love deep into the night. Hank had booked a trip for them on a fifty-foot catamaran called *Island Time* to the island of Bimini for the next day.

When they awoke on Tuesday, October 29th, Maggie felt calm and peaceful. She knew she loved Hank and had found the man of her dreams. Perhaps he could move to Vermont with her and they could own a little cabin in the woods, light fires in the winter when the snow piled up outside and watch little Hanks running around.

The two showed up for their voyage with Maggie wearing a red one-piece swimsuit with black circular Celine glasses and her straw hat, and Hank sporting some boardshorts and a half-buttoned-up white linen shirt. The week-long excursion to the Caribbean costed a pretty penny, but with all Maggie's savings from her modeling days, they could afford it.

The deck hand, Scooter, walked up wearing some zinc oxide strip on his tanned nose, and grabbed the couple's bags from Hank.

"Welcome aboard guys!" He helped Maggie up.

The Captain, Bob Dozer, swung around the mast and extended his hand to Hank. Bob, a golden-skinned Floridan reject wearing an unbuttoned white linen shirt just like Hank's and black roped Croakies on his Persol sunglasses, which dangled way down around his neck, was carrying a bottle of Pinot Noir in his other hand. "Come on guys, I'll give you the grand tour."

He took them into the galley and showed them the kitchen, then gave them a tour of the various rooms. In under an hour, the boat was off into a dazzling display of color along the horizon. A few dolphins followed alongside the boat and Maggie told Hank she had never felt this free before, not even in Vermont.

Scooter, who was also the chef, led them to a table at the rear of the boat where a crisp, clean white tablecloth greeted them. The two lovers sat down and Scooter brought the first dish out, a Mexican patterned platter full of freshly grilled plump shrimp. He poured them each a glass of red wine and they enjoyed a few of the shrimp. Then Scotty, as everyone called Scooter, brought out the lobster tails and a side of melted butter, freshly cut ripe mangoes and chicken liver pate with buttered toasties.

Maggie asked Hank what he thought about marriage and he said, "Between us, absolutely baby," and winked at her. She snuggled her face into his white linen shirt, while the rays of the sun pounded them.

23

RETURNING TO CAROLINE

A t the first light of dawn Tuesday morning, John and Angela ate breakfast in the lobby of the Chelsea Inn and checked out promptly. Paint finished or not, they were going home. On the way, they agreed to stop by the local hardware store, Bob's, and obtain some red brick dust.

After John explained to the grey-bearded boss who was wearing a patterned Florida shirt what he needed, the man acted like John was crazy, but said, "Okay."

He brought out three bricks the color of the Arizona skyline. "What do you want me to do with them, grind them down?" the man asked John.

"Sure, just grind them for me and toss the dust in a bag."

He studied John. "I have only had that request once before. You haven't been to see that crazy Voodoo Queen of Duval Street by any chance?"

"Yes, as a matter of fact, I have, and she said this would hex-proof our house."

"Well, she sent some moonbat to me trying to stop his wife from poisoning him with rat poison and he asked for this stuff. I guess it works, he didn't die. Still comes around, smiling like a rabbit in spring. This will cost you fifty dollars though," he said, as he began to turn the bricks to a fine powder.

"Fifty dollars, is that what everything costs around here?"

The man laughed, "You've been hanging around Duval too much."

When the man finished, John paid him and carried the red dust to the car. At their house, John dusted the front of their grey porch steps with the fine powder just like Miss Anne had suggested.

Then the couple entered the house to admire the painting executed thus far.

At that moment, Dexter paraded up the steps with Jason following him, with the intent to get his way or harm John.

Right as his foot passed the red dust, a diamond rattler cruising along the inside edge of the porch bit him on his big toe through his sandals, then darted off the porch by way of the stairs and disappeared into the neighbor's yard. The pain was unbearable, so Dexter hobbled down to the sidewalk where he collapsed in horror. Jason tried to help his friend.

Then he hollered out for help. Hearing the commotion outside, John and Angela rushed out, where they saw the old billionaire foe lying on the ground in pain.

He rushed over to Dexter's side and, forcing the energy through his palms, healed the rattlesnake bite. The positive energy seeped into the wound in an aural light and the whole area began to turn a healthy pink color again. In an instant Dexter was cured and the venom was neutralized.

Dexter begged John for his help with his ALS and John said, "Come inside," and helped him up. Jason followed them.

John sat down beside Dexter on the sofa, while Jason stood. With all the power in his palms John tried to heal Dex of the dreaded ALS a second time. This time, after a few minutes, Dex's expression changed from sullen to joyful and John knew it was working. Five minutes later, the pain was gone and Dex claimed he could breathe again, and hugged John.

John didn't know why he was able to cure Dex this time but not the first time, perhaps it was because he had abstained from coffee and cigars. Who knows?

Dex offered money, but John said no, he didn't want it. Happy to see the world again, Dex and Jason left, passing Pablo on the way out.

Pablo had come to put the final touches on the painting. "Hey my friend," he said. "Name is John, we spoke on the phone."

"Hola," he said, resting his hands on his hips.

"Hi, I am Angela, John's wife." Angela extended her hand. "The white looks fresh! We love it."

"Gracias."

"Any spooks while we were gone?" John asked.

"No, not really, just some rapping on the window, that's all. I thought it was a dog or something."

"Thank God!" Angela remarked. "I guess they were just after us."

"Is this house haunted or something?"

"Just a little," John said and winked at him.

"Let's get something to eat!" Angela said to John.

"Sounds good."

They unloaded the car in a light rain, placing their bags into the bedroom. Then, they headed out into the streets of Key West again on foot with tiny pellets of rain falling all around them. It felt good to walk in the rain again and not worry. John realized he loved his life much more without all the stimulants running through his veins all the time. Life was a gift and he knew that now.

They stopped at Blue Heaven restaurant whose slogan read, "You don't have to die to get here." The two laughed at the words, for they had experienced another side of life where death didn't have any meaning at all. Spirits live on in this world or the next.

They both ordered a Rooster Special of two eggs scrambled, spicy sausage, buttered grits and banana bread, and Angela asked for a coffee with cream... and John a decaf. When Angela's coffee came, John did not desire the slightest sip. His addiction was gone. And now his throat was feeling 100% cured as well.

While waiting for their food, John got a call from Pablo that the painting was finished, and John gave him the green light for the office to charge the card on file. Pablo locked up and left the key under the mat.

They ate and talked and when their bellies were full headed back home to their newly painted cottage.

"Doesn't the fresh paint smell so good!"

John agreed, "Yeah that and cut grass always do it for me!"

"Hey, let's raid the pantry for some dark Oaxacan chocolate to celebrate?"

"Sure," John said, "sounds like a plan."

That night, no furniture moved, but the ghost of Count Tanzler did appear, circling the room. This time it woke Angela, who screamed in terror at the sight of the shredded phantom. The rain fell hard outside and lightning cracked in the distance.

John hauled ass out of bed at the sound of Angela's scream. "What is it?" he said, rubbing his eyes.

"The ghost! Look!" She pointed to where the Count had been, but he was gone.

And this time John didn't see it, but he knew she wasn't lying, especially when she described the Count's appearance. He relayed to her that it was the same ghost he had seen in the cemetery the night he was stuffed in the coffin. "He's the one that has been moving our damn furniture around."

They slept in a terrified state, and the next morning woke to a bright sun. Lo and behold all the furniture in the kitchen was where it always was. However, they were both frightened by the appearance of the ghost and agreed to go see Miss Anne one more time.

THIS TIME, Miss Anne's shop was crowded with a slew of characters, all sitting around the front window waiting. John and Angela sat down beside a young kid with ruffled brown hair who could read minds, his mother said. John smiled and thought of his own gift, and how he hadn't really used it apart from with Dexter. Maybe he could finally write page 100 in his book and finish it without coffee or cigars, and he would also resume taking calls from patients who were ill and needed his help, working long distance from Key West. It was his destiny.

In a little while, the line cleared out and Miss Anne rushed them over. She was wearing aviator sunglasses today.

"Tell me how my babies are doing!" She fired a fatty Churchill cigar, took a long drag on it and blew the smoke towards John.

"We don't know, the ghost is still there, but the white helped. Things are better. At least, he's not moving furniture anymore," John said. "Whew, that smell. Guess what Anne? I don't want it anymore."

"Hahaha, good, it's about time."

"We saw him last night," Angela said. "Well, I saw him."

"I see, I see. What did he look like? Come sit down." The three sat. Anne continued smoking the cigar.

"It's that Count, Count Tanzler, he's the ghost haunting our house, Miss Anne," John explained.

"Good. Now, the only thing I have left for you is for you to free the ghost's soul while wearing the Solomon's Seal."

"Okay, tell us, just how do we do a thing like that?"

"There is a very special tree in Key West called the Kapok

tree, it stands mightily in front of the courthouse. This tree is a sacred tree whose branches can carry a soul from this world to heaven. Take some of the Count's dirt from around his cemetery plot and put it in a mason jar, then carry it back to Key West and bury it at right at the base of the Kapok tree, and you should be free of his spirit forever."

"Okay, that sounds easy enough," Angela said.

"Yes, only one problem though," the Madame leaned back in her chair. "The Count wasn't buried here. No, no, he was buried up in Tampa. He was so strange to everyone here, he had to flee Key West. You should take a road trip up there to his grave, get some of his soul dirt."

24

COUNT TANZLER'S GRAVE

Friday, October 30th

The graveyard appeared empty and neglected as John and Angela approached the iron gate, which creaked wickedly as Angela opened it. They combed over rows and rows of tombstones, until they reached a gravedigger who also happened to be named Carl. He didn't look like old pictures of the Count, so John thought nothing of it. John asked where Count Tanzler was buried and Carl pointed over to an area near a wide oak tree. When they reached the tomb, John kneeled, dug up some of the dirt in front of the Count's grave, unscrewed the mason lid and placed the soul dirt in with his hand.

"Well, now we have it," said to Angela, "let's take it back to Key West to the Kapok tree and set him free."

"Good, let's do it girl."

During the long drive back to Key West, the couple talked about the Voodoo princess and how she had helped them so much, and how painting their cottage white had mostly done away with the the Count's haunting of the house – or at least his freakish moving of the furniture. Now it was time to set his soul free and send him back home at the Kapok tree.

Angela researched the Kapok tree's symbolism on her phone while John cut through the state on I-75. Scrunched up in the passenger seat in one of her strange contortions that always amused John, she read how the Mayan dream tree was the most sacred of all trees to the Mayans, symbolizing the three levels of earth: the roots connecting to the underworld, the trunk representing life on earth and the branches extending to the heavens – and the thirteen layers of heaven the Mayans believed existed there. The tree was called *Ceiba pentandra* and was a tropical tree native to the Caribbean, Mexico, Central America, northern South America, and tropical West Africa. The Yaxche or "green tree", as the Mayans called it, was where they held their weddings. Fitting that the Count would be set free from his deranged love interest Maria Elena "Helen" Milagro de Hoyos and be united with God in heaven under the tree where people tied the knot. He would be bound, not to this world any longer, but to the next.

They rolled into Key West early the next morning around five a.m., and wasting no time, they headed straight down Fleming Street where they turned onto Whitehead. At 502 Whitehead, they stopped in front of the gorgeous Mayan dream tree.

A barefoot black man who introduced himself as Sandy, greeted them at the tree and asked if they needed help.

"What do you know about it?" John asked.

"Well my wife, Lilah, and I came here many years ago. I lead people. I founded the African Method Episcopal Church here."

"Oh well, so nice to meet you," Angela said, but John got the feeling from Sandy's clothes that he wasn't from here, or wasn't from this time at least. John instinctively knew he was some kind of benevolent ghost from the island there to help them.

John handed the jar to Sandy, who had a little trouble

unscrewing the lid with his left index finger and John saw the scar around it.

With an insight that transcended rational thinking, Sandy walked to the tree and said, "Here we go!" and threw the dirt up into the tree, where the wind carried it all the way to the top of the rustling leaves. In the distance they saw a ray of light break through the sky as the Count's soul disappeared into the magic of the rising sun. Then, Sandy told them, "That will do it for him," and smiled, before walking off toward the sun just peeking over the horizon in the distance.

25

THE CATMAN OF KEY WEST

Halloween day, John and Angela picked up Howlin' Wolf before returning to their house, and he howled like a king from the backseat. That night they slept like babies for the first time since the ghosts and wretched dreams first appeared and even Howlin' Wolf got a spot in the bed for once, something John was strongly opposed to.

The next morning, the lovers woke to the most brilliant light streaming through their windows. The white walls seemed to make everything luminous, filling the house with joy and kindness.

John walked into the kitchen wearing a white t-shirt and baby blue boxers, scratching his head. Angela followed shortly after, and there was no reformation of the chairs or barstools. Everything was as it should be.

The two lovers smiled while preparing fried rice Thai-style for breakfast. Angela served a heaping portion for Howlin' Wolf who wagged his long tail enthusiastically. Angela made herself some coffee like always, and John drank a glass of freshly squeezed orange juice he made himself. An abrupt call buzzed through for Big John from an officer, informing him that the public intoxication charges were being dropped.

"How so? I mean just like that?"

"Yeah, you got a friend in high places. Hank Judge signed off on it, he was the arresting officer. You can thank him later."

The two clapped and hugged, and John spun Angela around in his arms. Howlin' Wolf barked in joy. Then they agreed to go to the beach for the day to get some sun.

While they bronzed in the sun at the Southernmost Point, their troubles truly felt behind them. They toasted to life, sipping their Mojitos in the sun. During their long conversation Angela told John how grateful she was for him, and he told her he appreciated her too.

After getting some good rays, they headed on down to Mallory Square to watch the Frenchman Dominique Lefort, also known as the Catman of Key West, perform with his flying cats. Angela and John admired the show as the cats leaped through burning rings of fire, walked on tightropes and finally one cat even strutted on its hind legs. In the middle of the show, John's bird, the macaw, appeared and flew through one of the burning rings. Everyone in the audience was awestruck, and John and Angela realized that they had walked through the fires of hell lately and come out the other side, better for it.

When the show concluded, the two began the walk home, stopping at a cart to buy some cut coconuts. Jimmy Buffett's "Barefoot Children in the Sand" was playing on an old beat-up boom box. The coconut seller, clearly a native Conch, said, "Thanks Bubba" to John and that was all John really needed, confirmation that he was a local in the eyes of a local.

That ended the evening for the pair, who wandered on foot back home to their island home. And John's ghosts, his abuse of cigars and coffee were fading from them too.

The next day, on the first day of November, John sat down to a nice glass of iced mint tea with a spoonful of sugar, and wrote page 101 of his book. And he didn't stop there either, he continued writing for hours. He never broke once to smoke a Habano on the porch, and he found his writing was better for the first time in a while. He was more creative and could think more clearly.

26

VERMONT

Two months later, Maggie and Hank packed up the last box of his stuff and loaded it onto a moving truck. They said goodbye to the Key West cottage they had recently closed on, hopped in the truck and drove north to Applebury, Vermont.

After a long, icy drive up I-95 through Washington D.C. and Manhattan, the two pulled into Maggie's little hideaway in a Vermont blanketed in white snow. Two whitetails darted into the wood when Hank turned the engine off. And that first night to a romantic full moon and with a brilliant fire crisping in the bedroom, they made love in her French antique bed under her flannel sheets, with the intention to have a baby a girl who they would name Tao – after their spiritual paths had converged in a way no one could explain.

L.A. to Vermont to Key West, Maggie had seen it all. And Hank was relieved to be chopping wood every day. He even grew a lumberjack beard and spent his mornings reading John Muir by the fire, while sipping his black coffee instead of watching the bleeding U.S. news back on fire island. He decided to get a job as a forest ranger instead of a cop.

27

THE HITCHER

Two months after Maggie and Hank left for Vermont, Big John had packed Angela and his U-haul and he was speeding up the highway with sheets of rain blasting against the wide windshield of the truck. He hadn't been able to see through the weather in over fifteen miles.

After John finished his book *Healing Hands*, the couple had gotten pregnant and made the decision to move back to L.A. to be closer to family. Angela had left two days prior in their Land Rover with Howlin' Wolf, while John stayed behind to finish packing with some movers.

It was night; he had left the Keys three hours prior and was winding up the highway making his way towards I-10 slowly. 2,695 miles to go until he reached L.A. and he figured he could make the trip in forty-two hours, breaking it into many days. He had abstained from drinking coffee and was sipping on a water instead.

As the rain eased up a little, John saw a hitchhiker up ahead on the side of the road just outside of Key Largo. He was wearing a charcoal slicker with the hood obscuring his face and had his thumb out, old-fashioned style. This guy was soaked from head to toe.

John never dared pick up a hitcher, but with tonight's weather, he figured it couldn't hurt.

He shouldered the big truck over to the side of the deserted highway and stopped. The headlights spot-lighted the skinny fellow, who John reckoned was bagless, as he dropped his thumb and ran over to the passenger door, swung it opened and jumped in.

John held out his hand to the young man who had a thin, timeless face with dark indigo eyes.

"Big John."

"Amethyst," the guy replied, shaking his hand.

"Amethyst, like the stone?" John studied the young man.

"Yes, that's me."

"Is that the name your momma gave you?"

"I guess, it's the only name I have," Amethyst replied.

"Hahaha, alright man, works for me if it suits you. So, tell me where you are going?"

"To Texarkana, Arkansas. Can you take me there?"

"Sure," John agreed, "I'm going to L.A. I think Texarkana is on the way along I-40."

"Nice."

"Alright, let's ride."

John pulled back onto the road.

"So where are you from buddy?"

"There."

"Really wow, what are you doing way down here in the Keys on the road in a night like this?"

"Why are you asking so many questions?" Amethyst demanded.

"Whoa chill, didn't mean to punch a button there."

"You didn't. I just don't get it." The young hitcher seemed defensive. "Where are you from? What do you know?"

"I'm Big John from Los Angeles. My mom is Susan Hoover and my dad's name is Henry. I went to school at Santa Monica High. I can heal sick people with the palm of my hands. And that's about all you're getting out of me."

"Hold on," Amethyst said, "you need to pull over and wait for a minute. A deer is about to pass a mile up ahead."

John shook his head. "What? I am *not* stopping buddy, I got miles to peel, besides it's late man, I am trying to pull an all-nighter here. Where are you from, 'Frisco?"

"Pull over."

The teen was so insistent that John almost agreed.

"Listen Amethyst, I don't get it. I pick you up in the pouring rain and you immediately tell me to pull over. What's your deal man?"

"Okay," Amethyst sighed, "but we will hit a deer in a minute. Have it your way."

John didn't say anything and gripped the steering wheel tighter. He could hardly see through the field of rain obscuring his line of vision. He turned up "I Know You Rider" by The Grateful Dead, Live from May 5th, 1970, and sang along. At that moment, his phone bleeped in with a text message from Angela, who was already in L.A. waiting for him, and he reached over to read it.

Next thing he knew, they heard a loud thump as a goliath force impacted the front grill of the truck.

John swerved the steering wheel to the right and the truck veered off to the shoulder. The teen hardly startled. John was out of breath.

"I told you to wait."

John looked over at him wide-eyed and then back at the road, shaking his head.

"Was it a deer?"

"I guess."

The lights illuminated the path ahead of them.

John opened the truck door and stepped out into the rain.

Up ahead in the luminescent glow of the headlights, a whimpering deer lay on its side along the shoulder. John could feel the energy in his hands just at the sight of the animal, and slowly approached it to see if he might help. When he got to the deer, John could tell it was injured badly. The ribs broken, it was badly bleeding. John immediately went to work, placing his hands on the deer's stomach. Within five minutes, the deer frolicked, rose and raced off into the surrounding woods. John thanked God, walked back to the truck and hopped in.

The two traveled for a while. John could feel his stomach rumbling. At the sign of the first Denny's he pulled over and parked the truck.

"Hungry?" he asked the kid.

"I guess so."

"Good, let's eat."

The two got out and walked into the diner.

They sat down in a booth and a waitress named Big Lips (it read that right on the tag) handed them two laminated menus and asked what they wanted to drink. The boy ordered water, as did John. He had continued to abstain from all his treats since the hauntings in the Keys – caffeine, cigars and bad food – and he was hungrier than normal. Something about traveling on the road put miles on his stomach. It was always like that.

Miss Lips came back over with their waters and asked if they were ready to order.

John had spotted a double bacon cheeseburger and he felt that would soften the punch of the long night of driving he had ahead of himself, so he ordered one. The boy removed his hood and John saw his eyes clearly in the light for the first time. He knew why the boy was named Amethyst – his eyes really were amazing. Like something from another planet.

The woman didn't seem to notice, she wasn't the kind that

noticed anything. She could look right at something and not even see it.

The boy quietly ordered, "Just a few pieces of Wonder Bread, that's all."

"Okay, you want any jam or butter with that?"

"No, just the bread."

"How about toasted?"

"No just the bread will be fine."

When Big Lips left, John asked the boy why he only ordered bread.

"It suits me."

"Okay Wonder Boy, but you're going to get hungry later in the night when we are hauling tail up 95 you know. Might wanna get something with some cheese on it."

"No," insisted Amethyst, "just the Wonder Bread, that's all I ever eat."

"Just bread? Sheesh, I couldn't do that. I learned how to abstain from junk food years ago, everyone called me Big John I was so fat, and it was hard as hell to lose the weight, but living on just white bread, no way Jose." John withheld the information about the Romany gypsy who cured him of his bad food addiction and Miss Anne who just took him off cigars and coffee for the time being.

Amethyst sat there looking at John.

"So," John asked carefully, "tell me again, how did you see the deer we hit coming?"

Amethyst shrugged. "I always know what's getting ready to happen. Like your napkin, you are getting ready to lose it."

John looked at his napkin. "But wouldn't telling me about losing my napkin cause me to not lose it?"

"It could, but I can intervene to change the future by telling you, so that in telling you, it will happen. That's why I told you about the deer, so we could change the future, but you didn't listen to me because I am young."

At that moment, the waitress came and topped off John's water and a busboy walked past her, bumped into her fat rump, which hit the table, spilling John's water all over the place. The waitress apologized profusely as she picked up his soaking wet napkin too fast for John to even stop her.

Amethyst just smiled and watched John. The busboy mopped up the remaining water and when he left, Amethyst said, "See, you lost it, or it lost you. Either way, it's gone now, and I was right, wasn't I?"

"I can't believe it," John exclaimed, "but...but...what did you see, tell me?"

"I see it happening in my mind."

28

AMETHYST REVEALED

The two had been back on the road for hours and the rain was still coming down.

"I can't see anything." John said.

"I can though," Amethyst said, smiling. "I can see everything."

After another hour of listening to The Grateful Dead with John singing, the two were on I-75 when Amethyst ordered John to take the next exit. John agreed this time without blinking an eye. He had witnessed fate knock twice, first with the deer and second with the napkin, and he wasn't going to challenge Wonder Boy again. John took the exit.

"Where are we going?"

"I don't know yet. We just had to get off that road. Turn left."

John obeyed wearily.

"Turn left again."

"But that's going back in the other direction on the interstate, which makes no sense kid."

"Down and back like in football John. I can't tell you why, it's just what we have to do to stay safe."

"Jeez," John uttered, reluctantly taking the turn back south

towards Gainesville. By this point John was feeling uneasy, sick
to his stomach even. What did the kid mean, stay safe? Were
they in some danger? They drove along the interstate for about
three miles and then the boy ordered John to exit again. It was a
little late, and John nearly hit a car that was exiting behind him
as he cut across the white lines to make the exit.

"Dude give me a little more time, won't you?"

"I couldn't, I just now saw that you had to turn."

"Sheesh," John said, and sipped his water. Up ahead, the
boy asked him to turn into a gas station and park. John did as
he was instructed and the boy announced he had to take a
whiz.

"Hold up kid, tell me what's going on here. I need to know."

Amethyst sighed. "Look you don't know this, but I know
you. I am Carl Tanzler's great grandson. He sent me here to
protect you on your drive back to California, in return for
releasing his soul at the Kapok tree. Just now, I saw things
happening up ahead of us: stoplights, crashes, police sirens."

"Really? What the hell? The Count's great grandson?" John
thought for a minute. "Are you serious?"

"Yeah man, like why would I joke with you?"

"Okay, okay, but remember I got a serious schedule to keep
here. We can't keep turning around and stopping here and
going back all night. You got to take that whack back to 'Frisco
buddy. I mean how exactly do you do anything with this gift of
yours? I have a gift with my hands too. You saw me heal the
deer back there, right?"

"Yes, I saw, John. All Starseed children like us have unusual
gifts."

"Yeah yeah, I know about Starseeds. Never heard of one
that could see into the future like you though."

"There are others out there like me and you, hiding, waiting
for the day when they can come out into the world."

"Yeah I think you're right. I guess so."

At that, the kid jumped out and ambled inside the gas station. John was seriously thinking about pulling away and leaving the boy stranded there, but his hands just tingled like crazy at the thought of it. He was now along for the ride with the kid, like it or not. What was this turning around stuff, and where on earth were they heading now? Who was this strange kid standing in the rain outside of Key Largo from Texarkana, Arkansas? Wasn't Texarkana a small odd dot on a map on the Texas-Arkansas state line? The puzzling questions came fast and hard like the rain.

A minute later Amethyst came out with a loaf of Wonder Bread and got in the car. He took out one single piece of bread and ate it slowly. "You can drive friend."

"Okay," John said, as he shifted the truck into reverse. "Hey if I eat that bread, can I see like you?"

Amethyst smiled quietly. At the road, the kid pointed to the left and told John they had to take a back road all the way north, that the main road was littered with frogs.

"Littered with what? Frogs?"

"Yes, bullfrogs. Tons of them, and lightning is going to strike any minute all around us."

Waiting to turn left, the lightning poured from the sky in strikes, like a real lightning storm. John couldn't believe it. His head twirled around in disbelief, as the light lit up the night sky. He whipped his head towards the boy, who quietly looked forward, not saying anything. The kid was like a puppet of the future, only reacting when he had to give instructions about what he saw. Nostradamus, John thought.

After traveling on the bizarre back road for what seemed like an eternity, Amethyst asked John to take a right onto a narrow and heavily forested road. It looked just like something out of a Robert Frost poem, and John swore they were taking the road less traveled now. His mind wandered to how Robert Frost lived in Key West every winter but wrote poems about snow. That didn't make any sense to John. Did Frost summer in Connecticut? He wondered what he had gotten himself into, but curiosity gripped him now and he had to know who this strange young man was and what it all meant.

"So, tell me Amethyst, who are you really and where are we going? I have to get this truck full of furniture to Los Angeles and I don't really have time for any more bizarre detours."

"I am a messenger between this world and the next. And you, my friend, are going back to San Francisco in the Golden Gate State now, where Angela and you shall live, not L.A. Those days are over."

The End.

To Be Continued in Book 3: Big John and the Hitcher

GLOSSARY

Alonzo's Oyster House – A Key West fish-house established in 1947, now the best place to get oysters. Alonzo's is where Dan, John's flyfishing guide, gets drunk on dirty gin martinis after a long day of flyfishing.

Angela Hoover – John's Thai wife and a well-known musician. Loves the Grateful Dead, fresh coconut water and key lime pie.

Bien – A converted gas station Cuban eatery in Key West.

Big John Hoover – The world's best-known and least-recognized healing hands from Santa Monica, California. His parents are Susan and Henry of Long Beach and his wife is Angela, and the pair have a Northern Inuit puppy named Howlin' Wolf.

Big Sur – A small, beachfront mountain village on the Central Coast of California, known for its dramatic rocky cliffs and wild waves.

Bone Key – Another name for Key West Island, derived from the Spanish name Cayo Hueso.

Bubba – The oldest son in a Southern family, and Jimmy Buffett's nickname.

Bucci – A Cuban espresso, taken black.

Carl Tanzler or Count Carl von Cosel – (1877–1952) A German-born Key West radiologist who fell in love with a tuberculosis patient of his named Elena "Helen" Migaro de Hoyos (1909–1931). Two years after she died, he removed her corpse from the tomb and lived with it at his home for seven years.

Captain Tony's Saloon – Built in 1852 as an icehouse, it also doubled as a morgue. Then, it was a telegraph station and cigar factory after that. In the 1930s, Josie Russell bought it and turned it into Sloppy Joe Russell's Bar. Eventually, Josie moved the bar up the street. In 1958, Captain Tony Tarracino bought the bar and turned it into Captain Tony's Saloon, which is where musician Jimmy Buffett got his start – many nights paid only in tequila. It is purported to be haunted by the Lady in Blue, who was hanged at the infamous Hanging Tree that grows mysteriously in the center of the bar.

Cayo Hueso – Spanish name meaning "Bone Island" given to Key West by the Spanish, who found the bones of the Caluso Indians there in 1521.

Chelsea House Pool and Gardens – Historic inn in Key West supposedly haunted by its original owner, Mr. Delgado, who people believe was murdered in room 18 by his wife in the 19th century.

Cockfight – A despicable match between two roosters who are put together in a special ring known as a cockpit and allowed to fight. Usually bets are then placed on the birds. Outlawed in most places.

Cohiba Habano – One of the finest Cuban cigars, first created exclusively and only for Fidel Castro in 1966.

Conch Ceviche – National dish of the Bahamas and a favorite Key West plate. Uncooked, finely chopped conch is marinated in lime juice for hours and served with sea salt, freshly cut tomatoes, jalapenos, cucumbers, cut avocados and diced red onions.

Conchs – A name given to people born in Key West.

Cuban Coffee – An espresso served black with sugar.

Cuban Sandwich – Ham, roasted pork, swiss cheese, mustard and pickles served on fresh Cuban bread.

Day of the Dead – Also known as Día de los Muertos, Day of the Dead is a Mexican holiday where people gather to celebrate and pray for their loved ones who have passed on.

Dexter Wade – Big John's nemesis. Billionaire owner of Tech-tonic in Palo Alto, California, where John was taken by force to cure him of his paralysis in *Big John and the Fortune Teller*.

Dowsing Rods – Two L-shaped metal rods used by "dowsers" for finding water, divination and communicating with spirits. During this practice the user holds the rods in the hands, while a question is asked. Usually, if the horizontal rods merge towards the center when asking a "yes" or "no" question, the answer is "no", if they move apart, the answer is "yes".

Duval Crawl – When someone walks the whole length of Duval Street, bar hopping.

Duval Street – The "longest street" in the world because it stretches 1.2 miles from the Gulf of Mexico to the Atlantic. Most famous street in Key West.

Elena "Helen" Milagro de Hoyos – (1909–1931) A tuberculosis patient at Marine-Hospital Services in Key West who became the love interest of Carl Tanzler, her radiologist at the hospital. Carl removed her body from the tomb in 1933 and lived with it at his home for seven years.

Fantasy Fest – Key West Halloween-themed costume festival during the month of October, where many people have their almost nude bodies painted in artistic and humorous fashions at Parade Parlor Tattoo.

Ghost Hunters – An American reality TV show investigating the paranormal.

Grateful Dead (The) – Improvisational jam band led by lead singer Jerry Garcia based out of San Francisco, California, that rose to prominence in the 1970s. John and Angela's favorite rock group. Fans are referred to affectionately as Deadheads.

Hanging Tree – An infamous tree now standing in the center of Captain Tony's Saloon where over twenty criminals were hanged, including the Lady in Blue, which haunts the saloon.

Hank Judge – Key West Cop and Santa Monica High friend of Maggie May's.

Healing Hands – The book Big John Hoover is writing in Key West to teach other people how to heal maladies with their hands.

Hex-proof – Something that protects a person from being the target of spells.

Howlin' Wolf – (1910–1976) Stage name of Mississippi blues musician Chester Arthur Burnett, who wrote such songs as "Smokestack Lightnin'", "Killing Floor" and "Spoonful". He was a big man, weighing 300 pounds at 6 feet 3 inches tall. Angela and John named their Northern Inuit puppy after John's love for the singer.

Humidor – A box, usually wooden, for storing fine cigars that allows air and moisture to circulate to keep them fresh.

Ibrahim Ferrer – Famous Cuban musician and member of The Bueno Vista Social Club.

Juju – In French, *joujou* or "plaything", it is West African witchcraft.

Key Largo – A 1948 American film noir movie starring Humphrey Bogart and Lauren Bacall about a group of gangsters, one being Johnny Rocco (played by Edward G. Robinson), who hide out in a hotel in Key Largo, the first Florida Key, and seize control of the hotel during a hurricane.

Key Lime Pie – A luscious concoction of sugar, eggs and condensed milk.

King Solomon – Wisest and wealthiest king to ever live. King of Israel from 970–931 BCE.

King Solomon's Seal – Legend has it that Solomon's Seal was engraved on a ring made of brass and iron and given to Solomon by Heaven. It contained commands to good and evil spirits within it. These modern trinkets are used to ward off evil spirits. Miss Anne asks John to obtain one and wear it to send all the ghosts haunting him back to their graves.

Maggie May – John's first crush at Santa Monica High who became a highly paid model in L.A. under the stage name M.M. Ultimately, she ran away to Applebury, Vermont, where she works at a Psychic Store.

Marie Laveau – (1801–1881) The most famous Voodoo practitioner of all time, she lived in New Orleans and was very well known as a midwife and herbalist.

Miss Anne, the Voodoo Queen of Duval Street – Not much is known about Miss Anne, John and Angela's Voodoo reader. Dates of birth unknown, she arrived in Key West mysteriously one day in 1950 in the back of a dusty truck, with only one shoulder bag made from a coffee-bean canvas satchel, and has been there ever since.

Montgomery Martini – Key West resident Ernest Hemingway's favorite drink: 2 ounces of gin to 1/8th of an ounce of vermouth with a dash of orange bitters. Also called a 15:1 Martini.

Moon Ring – Created in 1975, the moon ring contains a liquid crystal that causes the ring that change color according to the temperature of the wearer's finger.

Mr. Delgado – 19th-century cigar baron who was purportedly murdered by his wife and haunts room 18 of their old home, which is currently an inn called the Chelsea House Pool and Gardens.

Nepenthe Beach – A quiet, isolated beach in Big Sur, California, where John and Angela first encountered John's white wolf in *Big John and the Fortune Teller*.

Northern Inuit Dog – Breed of Angela and John's dog, Howlin' Wolf, that resembles John's white wolf. The breed was the offshoot of a project in the UK from the 1980s to breed a dog that looked like a wolf.

Parade Tattoo Parlor – Famous for their elaborate nude paint jobs during Key West's legendary Halloween-themed Fantasy Fest.

Polydactyl – A cat that has six to nine toes on each paw, often popular with sailors who thought the cats brought them good luck. Sometimes known as Hemingway cats because the author had many of them at his Key West residence.

Red Stripe – A Jamaican beer.

Robert the Doll – A German made doll manufactured by The Steiff Company, given to Robert Eugene Otto, a Key West Floridian painter, by his grandfather when he was a boy. Legend has it the doll has supernatural powers such as moving objects, giggling and sensing who is around him.

Salty Dog – Slang for an experienced sailor.

Shadow Being – Ghosthunter lingo for a being of black energy (mass of the underworld) with no discernable gender.

Shine – Kermit "Shine" Forbes, a boxing coach who once took a punch at author Ernest Hemingway when he was refereeing a boxing match, but didn't connect. The two became friends and began boxing for fun at the writer's Whitehead Street residence.

Skeleton Key – Aka a bump key or 999 key, it is a special key that can be used to open any lock.

"Sloppy Joe" Russell – (1889–1941) Josie Russell was a Key West native rum runner, fishing-boat captain and Hemingway's friend and fishing partner for twelve years. He opened the famous Sloppy Joe's Bar on December 5th, 1933, the day Prohibition was repealed.

Tarot Cards – Playing cards used for divination and cartomancy by seers.

Techtonic – Palo Alto billionaire Dexter Wade's artificial breast implant company. Big John cured Dexter of his paralysis in *Big John and the Fortune Teller*.

Thai Panang – A Thai dish of thick red curry made with galangal, lemongrass, ginger and coriander, placed on a bowl of white rice donned with meat of choice.

The Catman of Key West – Frenchman Dominque LeFort performs at sunset on Westin Pier adjacent to Mallory Park with his 3 to 5 trained housecats, which jump through flaming hoops, jump from stool to stool and even walk on tight ropes.

The Cuban Coffee Queen – A Cuban coffee and food shack in Key West.

The Island of Bones – Another name for Key West Island, see *Caya Hueso.*

The Lady in Blue – A woman who stabbed her husband and two children to death; sentenced to death by hanging at the Hanging Tree in Captain Tony's Saloon, while wearing a blue dress.

Water Hands – Palm-reading terminology, water hands are one of the four hands, the other three being: earth, air and fire. Water hands are determined by long hands and fingers and indicate an intuitive, psychic personality in touch with their emotions.

DUKE TATE

BIG JOHN AND THE ISLAND OF BONES

Illustration by Bernard Lee

ABOUT THE AUTHOR

Duke Tate was born in Mississippi where he grew up surrounded by an age-old tradition of storytelling common to the deep South. He currently lives in Southeast Florida where he enjoys fishing, surfing, cooking Asian food and reading.

You can view his YouTube channel here and his author website here.

a amazon.com/Duke-Tate

g goodreads.com/9784192.Duke_Tate

f facebook.com/duketateauthor

twitter.com/duke_tate

ALSO BY DUKE TATE

Big John Series

Book 1: Big John and the Fortune Teller

With Ken Tate

The Alchemy of Architecture: Memories and Insights from Ken Tate

The Pearlmakers

Book 1: The Hunt for La Gracia

Book 2: The Dollarhide Mystery

Book 3: Gold is in the Air

The Pearlmakers: The Trilogy

My Big Journey

Returning to Freedom: Breaking the Bonds of Chemical Sensitivities and Lyme Disease

Gifts from A Guide: Life Hacks from A Spiritual Teacher

Translations

Gifts from A Guide: Life Hacks from A Spiritual Teacher - Spanish edition

Gifts from A Guide: Life Hacks from A Spiritual Teacher - Dutch edition

Big John and the Fortune Teller - Thai edition

Coming Soon

The Architect

The Cobbler

Big John and the Island of Bones

Quantum Healing: A Life Full of Miracles

Made in the USA
Monee, IL
12 November 2020

47303062R00080